"People usually are the happiest at home."

William Shakespeare

The Good Folks
of Lennox Valley
Spring & Summer 1998

by Kevin Slimp

Market Square BOOKS

©2017 Market Square Publishing, LLC.

Knoxville, Tennessee

The Good Folks of Lennox Valley
Spring & Summer 1998

©2017 Market Square Publishing Company, LLC.
books@marketsquarebooks.com
P.O. Box 23664   Knoxville, Tennessee 37933

ISBN10: 0-9987546-2-5
ISBN13: 978-0-9987546-2-8

Library of Congress: 2017906968

Printed and Bound in the United States of America

Cover Illustration ©2017 Market Square Publishing, LLC
by Danny Wilson
(dannywilson.com)

Author: Kevin Slimp
Editor: Cathy Sloan
Layout & Design: Kevin Slimp

Table of Contents

Preface

In 2009, I began writing about folks I have met throughout my life. I placed them together in my hometown of Lennox Valley.

I can still hear Marvin laughing at the domino table and Elbert Lee pitching a fit because I jokingly accused him of cheating for the hundredth time during a game.

In 2015, I began rewriting the story and released it as a syndicated column in hundreds of newspapers across America. Millions of readers join me each week, enjoying my memories.

Yes, the children's sermon really happened. There really is an Iris Long, a Helen Walker and a Brother Jacob, who still preaches in bare feet today. James Whedbee served an illustrious career as Methodist minister and district superintendent.

Glynn Vickers was a real Methodist minister, and his wife, Rona, is retired in Texas these days.

The list could go on. Some names have been changed. Some haven't. You can probably guess which are which.

For two years, my children, Ashley and Zachary, have listened to these stories each week. They sometimes laughed harder than I did. Earl Goodman joins me to read each story and makes suggestions before sending the columns to the editors. I have him to thank for reminding me I've misspelled Vera's name again. Cathy Pearce Sloan and Jean Henderson read, edited and re-edited these stories each week before they went out to newspapers. Cathy was the editor for this book.

Renowned illustrator Danny Wilson designed the cover of this book, as well as the caricature that accompanies my column each week. If he wasn't already famous, I'd say he might gain notoriety for his Lennox Valley work.

I've had friends and family, too many to mention, cheering me on as I completed this book. "Thank you" seems too little to say, but will have to suffice for now.

Working with Wil Cantrell, author of *Unafraid and Unashamed,* has inspired me to "up my game." I will be forever grateful to Wil and his wife, Rebecca, for their support and assistance throughout this process.

Finally, I want to offer my sincere thanks to the 200 community newspapers that carry my column. I have enjoyed hearing from your readers and laughing as they beg me to share "inside information" about election results and romances.

I hope you enjoy reading the adventures of my past as much as I enjoy sharing them with you.

Chapter One

Lennox Valley
My hometown

The home of my childhood rests snugly between two lakes with names descended from ancient Native Americans. It's been a while since I've had a mailing address in The Valley, and a lot has changed through the years.

A milestone occurred in 1993 when our first traffic light was installed on the corner of Main and Church Street. We still refer to that intersection as "Bearden's Corner," though no one is quite sure why.

At first there was quite a bit of excitement concerning the light. Some of the good folks of The Valley were pleased with the addition. Others, not so much.

The Lutherans, who occupied the northwest quadrant of "the corner," thought the light might encourage those who waited patiently to consider making a visit to one of their Sunday services. It was, it seemed to the Lutherans, the ultimate evangelism tool. Lutherans, not normally known for "street corner" evangelism or going door-to-door, were easily excited about increasing the flock in such a non-intrusive manner.

The Baptists, on the other hand, occupied the southeast quadrant of Bearden's Corner. There was great concern among members that the light would encourage drivers to consider a visit to the Hoffbrau, a German eatery that caused considerable chagrin among the Baptists - and some Methodists - who recognized it as the only establishment in Lennox Valley serving beer.

First Baptist Church put up quite a fight for two decades to keep "the Devil's brew" out of The Valley, but there were too many fine Lutherans and Catholics to make that last forever. Truth be told, there were probably a few Methodists who secretly voted for the referendum whenever it came up.

The 'Brau, as locals had come to know it, was the subject of at least six sermons at the Baptist Church since it first opened on the corner just after World War II. One of Brother Billy Joe's favorite sermons was titled, "You can't spell 'Devil' without 'Evil'," and referenced the 'Brau at least once during each of his three points. After a while, parishioners came to expect Brother Billy Joe's sermon on evil like clockwork every year, on the Sunday before Oktoberfest.

On the other hand, Father O'Reilly seemed to have no problem with the 'Brau. As a matter of record (if Vera Penrod's phone calls to the members of the Lennox Valley Auburn Hat Society can be considered "record"), the "good father," as she liked to call him, was often seen enjoying a Reuben sandwich, sauerkraut and a Miller Lite at the famed eatery.

What's more, Father O'Reilly seemed to have no interest in Vera's proclamations concerning his dining habits. Some thought he was taking a personal jab at Vera when, on the Sunday before Mother's Day, he led a homily titled, "The Devil wears a bright red hat."

Everybody thought the confrontation between Vera and Father O'Reilly would calm down in time. But hurt feelings sometimes hang on. With each passing year, the conflict seemed to gain steam. However, in 1998 something changed to shift Vera's attention to more important matters.

You see, the Methodist Church decided to appoint a new pastor in June 1998. Methodists do this every few years, and pastoral changes usually occur without too much fanfare. In smaller congregations like Lennox Valley Methodist, parishioners came to expect a new minister every two or three years. Usually, the exiting minister would explain that God was calling him to a new congregation.

When I was 15, I overheard J.D. Sanders, custodian at Lennox Valley Methodist Church, once say, "I remember brother Jackson saying the Lord had 'called' him to another place, before leaving the church in Springfield."

Lennox Valley Methodist was J.D.'s second job as a church custodian. Before retiring he was the full-time custodian at the big Methodist church in Springfield. He worked at the Lennox Valley church two days each week.

"I always thought it was funny," J.D. continued, "that the Lord always sends preachers a bigger salary when he 'calls' them to a new congregation."

Nobody would know about the appointment of a new pastor for another month or so, but the bishop and his cabinet – that's what Methodists call the denominational leaders who decide where ministers are appointed – had made the decision, and they would soon send word to the good folks at Lennox Valley Methodist Church.

It would be District Superintendent Jim Whedbee who would have the privilege of informing the expectant congregation. Like most Methodist superintendents, he had a successful career as a pastor before the bishop appointed him to "the district."

Most superintendents weren't particularly excited about their jobs after the luster wore off, but Reverend Whedbee did look forward to sharing information about appointments with excited congregations.

He would be careful to guard the secret concerning the new minister at Lennox Valley for a few more weeks. Sometimes changes occur at the last moment, meaning ministerial appointments have to be changed.

The new pastor's name was Reverend Sarah Hyden-Smith.

And everybody thought the traffic light was big news.

Chapter Two

Raymond Cooper
Renderings with Raymond

Elections have always been big deals in small towns, and Lennox Valley is no exception. Winning an elected office is one of the few ways to be a big fish in a community like The Valley. About the only other options were serving on a church board or getting your picture in *The Lennox Valley Hometown News*.

As I remember, 1998 was an especially contentious election. You see, it's almost impossible to get re-elected in a small town unless no one else wants to hold your office. The constable always seemed to run unopposed, as did the school board members, but other than those offices, there always seemed to be opposition.

Winning was anything but guaranteed in more important races. It's just too easy to make enemies when you've known your constituents most of your life. There never seemed to be a shortage of willing candidates for the mayor's office because there was always somebody who wanted to be a bigger fish.. Fortunately, Raymond Cooper was cast perfectly for the Moby Dick role. Well, almost perfectly.

It was well known that winning an election in Lennox Valley was much easier for a candidate who was a member of First Baptist

Church. First Baptist was the closest thing to a political machine in our town. With close to 20 percent of the good folks of Lennox Valley on its membership roll and, just as importantly, more than 30 percent of the town's voters, it was hard to win against someone with that many built-in allies. The Baptist hymn, "Victory in Jesus," could have been a campaign slogan, assuming Brother Billy Joe would have allowed such a thing.

Raymond, however, had a plan. A few years earlier, he had correctly predicted the upcoming boom in talk radio. He had begun listening to a nationally syndicated radio program based at a station in South Florida and quickly realized the potential of this "new" medium. The Florida host's listeners were mesmerized by his every word. Raymond figured if it worked in South Florida, it would work in Lennox Valley.

Cooper noticed that fans of the show believed anything uttered by the host. He was adored, and his listeners would have followed him to the gates of hell, had he made such a request. Fortunately, he hadn't.

At first, Raymond's station was primarily an outlet for sharing his off-the-wall social and political views. But as time passed, he quickly came to see there were additional advantages to owning the town's only radio station.

In 1993, Talk Radio 880 moved to an "around the clock" format, primarily filled with syndicated programming from faraway places. The good folks of Lennox Valley were fascinated with stories about UFOs, corrupt politicians and, sometimes, religious programming. It took a lot to fill 24 hours every day, and there wasn't much to do, other than watch TV or listen to the radio, much of the time.

The good folks of The Valley became familiar with evangelists like Todd Cecil of Branson, Missouri, and "Handsome" Rob Cantrell of Galax, Virginia.

The most popular show on 880 was *Renderings with Raymond*, which could be heard twice each weekday. The show aired live from noon until 3:00, then repeated each evening from 8:00 until 11:00. In time, the show gathered listeners throughout The Valley, and Cooper became a household name. Even folks who didn't particularly agree with Cooper listened to his show. After all, it was the only local programming in our town.

Helen Walker liked to say Raymond had a gift. She never went so far as to explain exactly what his gift was, but she was quite sure the Good Lord was smiling upon one of his favorite, as well as most popular, creations.

Vera Penrod had a love-hate relationship with Cooper. Depending on his stance at the moment, she could be his biggest ally or his most vocal foe. As long as he steered clear of making disparaging remarks concerning the Lennox Valley Auburn Hat Society, Raymond generally stayed on Vera's good side.

As many listeners as he drew, most folks still considered Raymond a political nut case. Cooper realized, however, that nut cases tend to attract other nut cases, and such was the case with his following. It didn't take him too long to realize that it only required 400 nut cases to win an election in The Valley, and that's just what he intended to do.

If he was going to win the mayor's race, beating the incumbent, "Silver Tongue" Dick Bland, and a few other yet-to-be-determined opponents, Raymond needed a hot button issue to get voters excited about the next election. He tested the waters with various ideas.

There was the "PG Rated Movie Controversy" of 1996 and the "No Halloween Debate" later that year. He quickly backed off the Halloween strategy when he began to realize October 31 ranked right up there with Christmas as a favorite holiday among the good folks of Lennox Valley.

Sooner or later, he was bound to stumble on the right issue, and beginning in February 1997, *Renderings with Raymond* became a hotbed of fiery conversation centered on the Federal Reserve

System. It was sheer genius. Sure, mayors of small towns have no influence on the Federal Reserve System. Nor did most people give it much, if any, thought. But Raymond knew he only needed 400 good folks of Lennox Valley to care, and care they did. The more he railed against the Federal Reserve, the more listeners became incensed that a government agency – an unelected government agency, at that – could sway so much negative influence over our community.

Heated debates concerning the system aired daily. Often, Cooper continued the show past its allotted time slot. There were important issues to discuss, and he was just the man to lead the discussion.

Raymond pressed the idea that egg prices had risen 72 percent in just four years, all due to inadequacies in the Federal Reserve System. Callers were furious about corrupt federal officials controlling their dairy prices. At that rate, eggs would soon be beyond the financial reach of much of The Valley.

In February 1997, no one knew that Raymond Cooper had his eye on the mayor's seat. But as the price of eggs continued to rise, along with his listeners' collective blood pressure, it was only a matter of time until Raymond officially threw his hat into the ring.

Chapter Three

Brother Jacob

"No shoes" church

In 1998, Brother Billy Joe Prather was universally recognized as the fieriest preacher in Lennox Valley, with good reason. Not a Sunday, nor a Wednesday night for that matter, passed at First Baptist Church without an altar call and at least two re-dedications by souls who had wandered astray, ultimately finding their way home during the last verse of "I Surrender All."

Brother Billy Joe was a graduate of Dallas Theological Seminary, and he had a real knack for preaching. He could shout to the Lord one moment, then shed tears over a lost sinner in the same breath. It was said his smile was so bright it lit the entrance to heaven.

Bob Dylan probably had no idea he was prophesying the future of Lennox Valley when he sang, "The Times They Are a'Changin'." The year was 1998, and changes were about to become a part of life in our small town.

One of the biggest changes to occur that year was the calling of Jacob Gehrig, direct descendant of Lou Gehrig, to serve as assistant pastor at Lennox Valley Lutheran Church.

It's funny what we remember about our childhood. I remember

my Methodist friends talking about a new pastor being appointed to their church. It seemed like Lutheran and Baptist ministers were "called." I used to think Lutheran and Baptist clergy sat by the phone, just in case a needy congregation called them. Eventually, I came to learn it was just the church's way of saying they got a new minister.

Assistant pastors might be the norm in bigger cities, but they were a rarity in Lennox Valley. First Baptist Church had an assistant on staff for as long as anyone could remember. The other churches in town were too small for such "gaudy, frivolous behavior." That all changed with the hiring of "Brother Jacob," as he liked to be called, in 1997.

The Lutherans were quite excited to have the descendent of a legend serving in their pulpit. He was young and a bit wet behind the ears, but Valley Lutherans were a loving, peaceful group, and they would help Brother Jacob fulfill his role as a shepherd of their flock.

While associate pastors at First Baptist Church were known to preach a sermon now and then, almost always during a Sunday or Wednesday evening service, Lutherans generally relegated their associates to working with the youth and visiting the sick. Sure, a Lutheran associate pastor might get to pray or assist with communion from time to time, but that was as far as they could hope to go while serving in the second chair.

That changed in 1998 after Brother Jacob attended a church growth seminar in Kansas City, Missouri, held at a famous Methodist "megachurch." Jacob was mesmerized by the event. The sanctuary was large enough to hold 4,000 worshipers. Every seat was filled during the seminar. Famous preachers led sessions in worship, preaching, visiting, writing books and more. There were Bible studies each morning before breakfast and each evening after dinner.

To hear Brother Jacob tell the story, his heart was strangely warmed at the conference, and he felt led to come back to Lennox

Valley and begin a "contemporary service" at his church. Contemporary services, usually with drums and electric guitars, were all the rage, as he explained, at Methodist megachurches. Jacob saw no reason they couldn't do wonders for the good folks at Lennox Valley Lutheran Church.

For 16 months, Brother Jacob led a group of 15 to 20 parishioners meeting in the fellowship hall of the church at 8:30 a.m. every Sunday. Unable to find drummers or electric guitarists to lead their service, these hearty early risers made do with a young junior college student who came home on weekends to play the keyboard for their flock. It wasn't a Methodist megachurch, but Jacob felt he was making an impact, just the same.

At least two things were different about Brother Jacob's preaching style. First, he never wore shoes when he preached. It was bare feet every Sunday, even in the winter.

He would wear shoes, however, when leading a funeral. Apparently Thelma Biggers set him straight about that while making preparations for her late husband's funeral. Brother Jacob played it safe at funerals after that.

He said preaching in bare feet had something to do with Moses and a burning bush. We just took his word about that. I suppose if bare feet were good enough for Moses, they were good enough for Brother Jacob.

Second, Brother Jacob always used a paraphrased version of the Bible when preparing his sermons. Paraphrased versions are the writer's interpretation of what the scripture means, rather than a literal translation of the original Hebrew and Greek. *The Living Bible* is an example of a popular paraphrased version in the late 20th century.

He picked up the habit in seminary, when he learned he could actually understand the *Good News Bible* better than *The Lutheran Study Bible,* the translation preferred by his professors. By definition, a paraphrase is easier to understand, compared to a translation like the *Revised Standard Version* or *The Lutheran Study Bible.*

During his first year in seminary, Jacob was scolded by his advisors who learned of his preference for using a paraphrased version of scripture. Jacob learned to hide his less favored Bible from his fellow seminarians and professors, but he brought it to Lennox Valley where he often used it during sermon preparation.

There were times when that was problematic, as Lutherans preach from the "Lectionary," meaning they use prescribed Bible passages each week in their services. The idea behind the Lectionary is to work through the entire Bible, from Genesis to Revelation, in worship each year.

Perhaps the most memorable such problem occurred one Sunday when Brother Jacob was preaching in the main worship service while the senior pastor was on vacation. This was his first opportunity to preach in the sanctuary at "big church," and he worked feverishly to be sure he was prepared for the momentous occasion.

The Lectionary passage this particular Sunday came from Psalm 50, verse 8. In the Lutheran Study Bible, the verse had something to do with not removing oxen from a neighbor's field. In Jacob's paraphrased version, however, the scripture read, "I will take no bull from you."

"Pastor" Jacob was never allowed to use his paraphrased Bible again after that Sunday.

Chapter Four

Egg Wars!
The feds take control

Saturdays from April through September were always busy on Bearden's Corner. That's when the Farmers Market came to Lennox Valley, and with no malls or fancy shopping centers to speak of, the Farmers Market was the place to see and be seen.

You could count on the usual vendors each week. There were local farmers selling corn, tomatoes and potatoes from the backs of their trucks, housewives who had spent their weeks preparing candles and other assorted crafts for potential customers, and almost always two or three community organizations that set up tables under tents bearing the name of Massengale's Mortuary, located 16 miles to the west in Springfield, the county seat.

Lennox Valley wasn't big enough for its own funeral home, so the Massengale family was more than happy for folks to see its name emblazoned on tents bearing displays by the Cubs Scouts, Veterans of Foreign Wars, and the Lennox Valley Auburn Hat Society, just to name a few. However, these weren't getting their usual attention this Saturday in early May.

You see, like many big events, there was planning and structure that went along with the weekly Farmers Market. Vendors and community organizations submitted requests and were assigned spaces by Vera Penrod, who not only served as president of the Lennox Valley Auburn Hat Society but also served as secretary of the Spring County Chamber of Commerce.

Vera took her duties very seriously. She remembered her mother quite often quoting Eleanor Roosevelt in saying, "With freedom comes responsibility." Vera was anything but irresponsible.

There weren't many avenues to gain power in a small town like Lennox Valley. As both president of the Auburn Hat Society and secretary of the Chamber, Vera was probably the most powerful woman in town, and she was more than happy to bear the burden of responsibility.

On this particular Saturday, there was more excitement than usual at the market. It seems there was a new tent at the far end past all the usual vendors, and as Vera Penrod skillfully noted, no one had reserved that particular space. Even more concerning, the tent didn't bear the Massengale nameplate. Something was amiss, and Vera was about to get to the bottom of the growing commotion.

At first, Vera was chagrined when she saw Marvin Walsh sitting underneath the tent behind a folding table, wearing denim bib overalls he recently purchased at a second-hand clothing store in Springfield. She was about to tell Marvin to pack up his stuff and come back another Saturday, when she saw the hand-lettered sign taped to the front of Marvin's table:

Save our eggs!
Stop the Federal Reserve System

Raymond Cooper, owner of The Valley's only radio station and host of *Renderings with Raymond* every weekday from noon until 3:00, grinned as he saw the would-be confrontation. He held his response for a moment, then was pleasantly surprised as he heard Vera tell Marvin, "It's good to have such fine, civic-minded individuals taking a stand for Lennox Valley."

A sly grin made its way across Cooper's face. It seemed like his scheme was working. If the most powerful woman in town had been swayed by his radio program, surely others were, as well.

And that, as they say, was that.

Raymond continued down Main Street, being sure to compliment the attire of each potential female voter he passed. "Memories last," he often reminded himself. They would surely remember his words of kindness.

A half block east, toward the red light, Elbert Lee Jones, one of the more prominent farmers in the area, was selling eggs out of the back of his truck. Raymond Cooper slyly grinned again as he noted the price of a dozen eggs had risen a nickel over the previous Saturday.

Callers to his show would be plenty over the next week. With egg prices continuing to "skyrocket," he was sure of that. Yes, this was going to be a good week for *Renderings with Raymond.*

NEW COLUMN: The Good Folks of Lennox Valley

by Kevin Slimp

The home of my childhood rests snugly between two lakes with names descended from ancient Native Americans. It's been a while since I've had a mailing address in "The Valley" and through the years a lot of things have changed. In 1993, a traffic light was installed at the town's main intersection, Bearden's Corner.

At first there was quite a bit of excitement concerning the light. The Lutherans, who occupied the northwest quadrant of "the corner" thought the light might encourage those who waited there to consider dropping by. It was the ultimate evangelism tool.

The Baptists, on the other hand, occupied the southeast quadrant of Bearden's Corner. There was great concern among members that the light would encourage drivers to consider a visit to the Hofbrau, a German eatery that caused considerable chagrin among the Baptists - and some Methodists - who recognized it as the only establishment in Lennox Valley that served beer.

The "Brow," as locals had come to know it, was the subject of at least six sermons at the Baptist Church since it first opened on the corner just after World War II. One of Brother Billy Joe's favorite sermon's was titled, "You can't spell Devil without 'Evil,'" and referenced the Brow at least once during each of his three points. After a while, parishioners came to expect Brother Billy Joe's sermon on evil every year - on the Sunday before Octoberfest.

On the other hand, Father O'Reilly seemed to have no problem with the Brow. As a matter of record (if Vera Pinrod's phone calls to the members of the Lennox Valley Auburn Hat Society can be considered "record"), the "good father," as he liked to call him, was often seen enjoying a Reuben Sandwich, sauerkraut and a Miller Lite at the famed eatery. What's more, Father O'Reilly seemed to have no interest in Vera's proclamations concerning his dining habits. Some thought he was taking a personal jab at Vera

The good folks of Lennox Valley first appeared as a weekly column in 59 newspapers in August, 2015. By 2017, hundreds of newspapers were publishing the story each week.

Chapter Five

Turkey Shoot

Something "fowl" is in the air

At last count, not that there is an official count of such things, there were six vegetarians living in Greater Lennox Valley in 1998. They included Billy and Wilma Perkins, who had been vegetarians for as long as anyone could remember, and their two children, Zachary and Ashley. That left two others.

The fifth was a junior at the local high school, Sarah Goolsby, who declared her vegetarianism during a stand-off with her mother. The argument started out as an innocent conversation about current events, but it somehow curved into an intense discussion about the Federal Reserve System.

It seemed like a lot of arguments in my hometown that year revolved around that mysterious branch of the federal government. Concern over the Federal Reserve was causing much friction among friends and families throughout The Valley. The conversation between Sarah and her mother quickly took a nosedive before ending as young Sarah professed her newfound concern for all living creatures, vowing never to touch meat again.

Her mother assumed her eating habits would return to normal before long, but Sarah was showing no signs of abandoning her meatless diet.

Vegetarian number six was Juliette Stoughton. Juliette, like many 40-something single women, originally had other plans for her life. But life is funny, and things don't always turn out as planned.

A year earlier, Juliette realized her true love lived far away from her home. She was certain she and Chris Roadhouse were soulmates, and soulmates shouldn't be subjected to things like distance and time apart. So in an act of passion, she packed most of her belongings and moved to Lennox Valley, where she could be forever with her soulmate and lifelong partner.

Unfortunately, it is often the case that soulmates find other soulmates, and eight months into the engagement, Juliette found herself alone in a place where she didn't know anyone.

Juliette soon realized that she had lost a part of herself since moving to Lennox Valley. Back home, she was involved in several causes, but in Lennox Valley, she had barely gotten out enough to know what, if any, causes needed her energy. She had no friends, and there was no prospect of Chris coming back.

So she sat. She sat and thought of what might have been. She imagined Chris Roadhouse in a new place with a new soulmate. She had many sleepless nights coupled with days she didn't leave her bed at all.

That changed in May of 1998 when Juliette picked up a copy of the October 15, 1997, issue of *The Lennox Valley Hometown News*. She found the weekly paper underneath a phone book that hadn't been touched in seven months, and for no reason, she glanced over the community calendar on page one.

That's when it happened. As she perused the various potluck dinners, Ruritan Club announcements, VFW meetings and Auburn Hat Society events, she saw it. Right there, on page one, printed in the blackest ink she had ever seen: "November 15: First Baptist Church Men's Annual Breakfast and Turkey Shoot."

She didn't know which made her angrier, the idea that people actually went out on a Saturday morning and shot turkeys in cold blood after gorging themselves with pancakes, sausage and who-knows-what in the church fellowship hall, or the sheer audacity to hold such an event, as cold-blooded and grotesque as it was, for men only.

For those of you who have never participated in a turkey shoot, it's probably the right time to explain something about this centuries-old activity. No turkeys are shot. At least, not in the last hundred years. Originally, men gathered with their weapons and shot at live turkeys, but things advance with time, and by the 20th century, turkey shoots evolved into shooting at paper targets with shotguns brought from home. The prize for the winning shooter, by the way, was a frozen turkey from Valley Country Store.

Unfortunately, Juliette didn't take the time to research the intricacies of a modern turkey shoot. For the first time in a long time, she found a cause to stir her emotions. In the shadows of her small dining room, Juliette began jotting ideas on paper.

First, she would need allies, others who would be as chagrined as she was about this horrid practice. That should be easy. After all, what normal person would feel right about shooting fowl on the grounds of a place of worship? Something seemed incredibly wrong about the practice.

Next, she would need a way to express her concerns to the masses. Perhaps Raymond Cooper's daily radio program would be the opportunity to begin her campaign. She didn't know Raymond, however, and she would soon learn he wasn't as averse as she was concerning animal sacrifices in holy places.

Finally, an event would be needed. Something to gather the troops. Letters to the editor? Certainly, but that would not be enough. A full-page ad in *Hometown News*? Again maybe, but still not enough.

That's when it came to her. It was time for a protest. And what better place to protest than the site of the murderous event, First Baptist Church.

Or maybe a march. Perhaps she could gather enough concerned citizens together to march outside First Baptist Church on a Sunday morning. This could be dangerous.

Oscar Wilde once said, "An idea that is not dangerous is unworthy of being called an idea at all."

Juliette was convinced she had discovered an idea worthy of Oscar Wilde.

Yes, Juliette Stoughton had found her cause.

Chapter Six

Lennox Pace of Life
Not as slow as outsiders think

I like to tell people that Lennox Valley rests in a lovely place where two mountain ranges meet. The truth is there are no mountain ranges. At least not within a few hundred miles of Lennox Valley. The area was first settled in the mid 1800s by European immigrants in search of a better life. What they found was land that seemed fertile for farming, although the winters were considerably harsher than what they were used to back home.

It wasn't the temperature so much. The wind, which never seemed to rest in the winter and spring, made this a challenging place to call home.

But home it was. And soon the beginnings of a town square started to take shape. The first church, All Saints Catholic Church, was built. The Methodists and Lutherans weren't far behind. Within a couple of decades, the Baptists had also found their way to The Valley.

A livery and general store were the first businesses. Other businesses developed in time. By the 1840s, Main Street was a hub of activity with a town barber shop, a diner, a newspaper, and even a jail.

Lennox Valley wasn't the original name of the community. The first European settlers called it Varnyahem (from "Var nya hem"), which in their native language meant "our new home."

In the 1870s, a banker took up residence in the village and soon owned a sizable portion of the town. He had two sons when he arrived, and soon a third was born. Eventually, he and his wife celebrated the birth of their daughter, Lennox.

To this day, no one is sure how the village of Varnyahem became the town of Lennox Valley. Old-timers repeat various tales they heard from their parents and grandparents. One particularly humorous version claims the banker agreed to pay for signs that would adorn both entrances to the village. When the signs were unveiled, they bore the name Lennox Valley. The local citizenry, being the kind, timid people they were, decided to not make a fuss.

Another story, more likely true, finds the banker making major contributions to both of the town churches in honor of his beautiful daughter. The pews and stained glass windows adorning All Saints Catholic Church are still in place to this day. And, according to this story, the thankful villagers renamed the town in honor of young Lennox.

Whatever the real story behind the name, Lennox Valley does not sit in a valley. Nor does it rest near any mountain range. It is a quaint place, though, and a lovely place to call home. There are four churches, a town square, the Hoffbrau (where one can find a fine Reuben sandwich), a Ruritan Club, a VFW post, Cub Scouts, and thirteen hundred and forty souls who call it home. While the rest of the country seemed fixated on *Friends* and *The X-Files* in 1998, the most popular TV show in The Valley was *Walker, Texas Ranger*.

To outsiders, life moved very slowly in Lennox Valley. But with a traffic light on Bearden's Corner, a new Methodist pastor to be announced any day, discussions surrounding the Federal Reserve System reaching near-fever pitch, and a yet-to-be-announced protest of the First Baptist Church Annual Men's Breakfast and Turkey Shoot on the horizon, life in my hometown was anything but slow in April 1998.

Yes, that pretty much describes the place I grew up. Looking back, Lennox Valley may have been the most exciting place on earth in 1998. More about that later.

The Good Folks of Lennox Valley

A few of the places you can find The Good Folks

- The Greenville Standard, Greenville AL
- Your Community Shopper, Ardmore AL
- The Elba Clipper, Elba AL
- The Fairview Observer, Fairview AL
- Wakulla News, Crawfordville FL
- Early County News, Blakely GA
- Bryan County News, Richmond Hill GA
- Coastal Courier, Hinesville GA
- The Georgia Post, Roberta GA
- Wright County Monitor, Clarion IA
- Denver Forum, Denver IA
- The Breda News, Breda IA
- Jesup Citizen Herald, Jesup IA
- Missouri Valley Times, Missouri Valley IA
- Lake Mills Graphic, Lake Mills IA
- Belmond Independent, Belmond IA
- The Power County Press, American Falls ID
- The Paper of Montgomery, Crawfordville IN
- Daily Republican Register, Mount Carmel IN
- The Vincennes....
- ....
- ....
- ....

- Arlington Citizen, Arlington NE
- Bottinau Courant, Bottineau ND
- Devils Lake Journal, Devils Lake ND
- Grant County News, Elgin ND
- Lakota American, Lakota NDG
- rant County News, Elgin ND
- Cherokee Messenger & Republican, Cherokee OK
- Kiowa County Democrat Snyder OK
- Newkirk Herald, Newkirk OK
- The Purcell Register, Purcell OK
- The Twin-City News, Batesburg-Leesville SC
- The Index-Journal, Greenwood SC
- Wagner Post Wagner SD
- Stickney Argus, Stickney SD
- The Standard, White Lake SD
- Timber Lake Topic Timber Lake SD
- Miner County Pioneer Howard SD
- Lake Andes Wave, Lake Andes SD
- Parkston Advance, Parkston SD
- Central Dakota Times, Chamberlain SD
- Vermillion Plain Talk, Vermillion SD
- ....
- ....
- ....
- ....
- ....
- ....

Chapter Seven

Hometown News

Cooper wages war

Small town news is a bit different from what you might find in big cities. Murders, bank robberies and other violent crimes weren't to be found in The Valley, but that didn't mean the local newspaper, *The Lennox Valley Hometown News*, was short on breaking stories. The editor, Iris Long, just had to be a little more creative than her metro newspaper counterparts in sniffing out front page stories.

In March, 1998, the headline on page one read, "New John Deere Spreader Just Arrived in The Valley." While a new spreader might not be front page news far away in New York City, or even 16 miles down the road in Springfield, farming equipment was big news in Lennox Valley, as a good portion of the local economy came from dairy, poultry, corn, and other products from farms.

When the local psychic, Madam Zorra, was arrested in 1996, the headline read, "Local Psychic Arrested: She didn't see it coming." Iris loved a catchy headline, and she got a good chuckle out of that one, even if it did get by many of her readers.

Fortunately there are usually Friday night games of one type or another, letters to the editor, ads for the local hardware store and back page advertisements for Honest Emmit's Used Autos to fill the pages. And if the news wasn't always interesting, it was generally good for a laugh or two.

As much as Iris had a way with headlines, on occasion, it was the wrong way. Like in 1996, when she penned: "Stolen Painting Found by Tree."

It wasn't until Jessie Orr, waitress at the Hoffbrau, pointed out the faux pas to her old friend that Iris realized what everyone was laughing about as she sat in her regular booth and munched on the Wednesday special of country fried steak, mashed potatoes, okra and a roll.

Most Valley residents still remember her front page headline from 1986: "Red Tape Holds Up New Bridge." Iris especially enjoyed that one.

Everyone in Lennox Valley understood the power of the press. It was a good idea to stay on Iris Long's good side. At 76 years, Iris had been in the news game for a long time, and she didn't "put up with foolishness," as she often reminded folks.

She liked to quote Mark Twain, who is often credited with saying, "Never quarrel with a man who buys ink by the barrel." Iris would change "man" to "woman " when she quoted Twain, however.

More than once since buying Talk Radio 880 in 1993, Raymond Cooper learned this lesson about ink the hard way. As owner and host of the only radio station in town, Raymond found ways to butt heads with Iris Long with increasing regularity. This became more evident since his rantings concerning the Federal Reserve System began in 1997.

Iris, like most veteran journalists, saw right through Raymond's "shenanigans," as she liked to call them. She wasn't sure if Raymond's Federal Reserve diatribe was just his way of gaining listeners, or if, as she suspected increasingly with each passing day, he had a more sinister ulterior motive.

Uncovering sinister motives is a common practice among journalists, and Iris had uncovered more than her share. Cooper wasn't fooling her by any stretch of the imagination. She just wanted to figure his angle. "What is he up to?" she would ask herself time and again.

Raymond, concerned that Iris's snooping would hurt his secret plan to enter the upcoming mayoral race, waged his own misinformation war against *The Hometown News*. He liked to tell his listeners that Iris had it in with the federal government, and it was rumored she had a relative on the Federal Reserve Board.

"I'm not sure," Cooper would shout into the microphone, "if she is just making this up, or if she is falling hook, line and sinker for whatever her friends in the federal government are feeding her!"

Temperatures were rising in Lennox Valley, and with the mayoral campaign getting ready to kick off, the Methodist district superintendent coming to town to announce the name of the new pastor, and Juliette Stoughton's plans to hold a protest at First Baptist Church, there would be no cool temperatures on the horizon as April 1998 came to an end in my hometown.

Chapter Eight

Methodist Ministers
They come and go

As April moved aside for May, the good folks of Lennox Valley had no idea how their world was about to change on Monday, May 4. On Talk Radio 880's *Renderings with Raymond*, callers were equally divided between two topics of vital importance.

The first had to do with a book making headlines in Europe and promising to take American youth by a storm. "Harry Potter," barked the first caller, Martha Jean Bratton, "is of the Devil and has no place in the hands of any self-respecting young person!"

News from Europe and seen on American newscasts described a book filled with wizards, magic and all sorts of evil activities not appropriate for the young folks in Lennox Valley. Host Raymond Cooper listened with great empathy, and his steady words calmed most of his faithful listeners.

"I feel certain," he told his listeners, "that enthusiasm for this 'Potter' character will wane soon enough." He added, "How many teenagers do you know who like to read? Mark my words, no one will remember Harry Potter by this time next year."

As for the second critical topic, the plight of the Federal Reserve System, which took up much of the next three hours, Raymond felt less confident. With "insiders" like Iris Long "fanning the flames in support of the government," Raymond noted with a sly grin not seen by his listeners, "the Hoffbrau raised the price of a Denver omelet from $3.25 to $3.29 over the weekend. If that's not proof of the havoc resulting from federal mismanagement," he shouted into the microphone, "I don't know what is!"

Callers were in a frenzy. If inflation kept up at this pace, eggs prices would soon be out of control. Fortunately for Raymond, listeners couldn't see his smile as he discussed their mutual plight.

Egg prices were soon to make way for other events unfolding just across town. The big news of May 4 didn't happen until 3:05 that afternoon, just after the show went off the air.

Diane Curtis, chair of the Lennox Valley Methodist Church Pastor-Parish Committee, had just turned off the radio when she heard her phone ring in the kitchen. The call was from Reverend James Whedbee, Springfield district superintendent of the Methodist Church.

Methodists, you see, don't select their own ministers like most Protestant denominations. Their pastors are assigned by bishops, and word is sent to the individual congregations through district superintendents. It's a long tradition going back to the days of "circuit riders" who traveled early America on horseback, constantly moving from one church to the next to make sure everyone received the sacraments on a steady basis.

"Mrs. Curtis," began the soft-voiced superintendent, "I'm calling with good news."

"Oh, really," she said, obviously excited. "What's that?" she asked.

Reverend Whedbee continued, "After prayerful consideration, we have selected a new pastor for Lennox Valley. As you're the chairperson of the PPR committee, I wanted you to be the first to know."

Diane had been on pins and needles for weeks, wondering

who the new pastor would be. Like everyone else at the Methodist Church, she hoped for a powerful orator with a strong singing voice and, if the Lord felt especially gracious, a wife who played piano.

Wives who played piano were very popular in small town congregations. Reverend Vickers had been very popular during his three years, and his wife, Rona, was a skilled pianist. However, in a congregation as small as Lennox Valley, three years was about as long as a minister stayed before either being sent to a larger congregation or retiring.

Diane envisioned a tall, handsome minister, probably in his early 40s, although most pastors at Lennox Valley Methodist were either fresh out of seminary or nearing retirement. His sermons would last 15 minutes, no more. Yet those 15 minutes would stir the hearts of parishioners and fill the altars with new converts.

Some Methodists in The Valley were secretly jealous of the Baptists, who seemed to keep their preachers for decades. They were resigned to the fact, however, "that's not the Methodist way."

"I suppose," Diane thought on more than one occasion, "it's better to have a preacher fresh out of seminary than one who drones on for hours on end."

One good thing about being Methodist was the certainty of beating the Baptists to the eating establishments after church, whether at the Hoffbrau, Betsy's Diner, or one of the many dining establishments in Springfield.

"The Reverend Sarah Hyden-Smith is being appointed to Lennox Valley," Reverend Whedbee uttered, then continued, "and her first Sunday will be June 14."

There was a long pause before Diane responded, "Did you say 'Sarah'?"

"Yes," repeated the superintendent, "Sarah Hyden-Smith. She is very excited about being appointed to your congregation."

The district superintendent mentioned that Diane's committee should start making plans to welcome the new pastor.

"Perhaps a potluck meal after her first service," he suggested tacitly. "Some music might be nice. Maybe someone could play piano," he added.

Diane wisely held back from responding with her first instinct, "I'm guessing the new pastor's wife doesn't play piano." Instead, she replied, "Yes, I suppose we should."

As Diane Curtis hung up the phone, Iris Long, editor of *The Lennox Valley Hometown News,* penned what she thought would be her next front page story. It had something to do a new grain elevator off Highway 11.

Like much in Lennox Valley, that was about to change.

Chapter Nine

Stop the Press!

Celebrity evangelist bumped from front page

Todd Cecil, host of Revival Flames Ministries of Branson, Missouri, was just about the biggest celebrity to make an appearance in Lennox Valley during my childhood and early teen years. He was a fixture on Sunday morning television since the 1970s, and my dad and I watched the famed evangelist as we waited for the rest of the family to get dressed for church each week.

I can still hear the opening song from the weekly show, "Revival Flames are burning, the winter frost is gone."

It might be hard to imagine a similar scene today, but small town America moved a little slower during my teenage years. Sunday mornings, for instance, revolved around TV while waiting for everyone to finish dressing for church.

At 5:30 p.m. on Monday, May 4, 1998, Iris Long had just created a headline for the Wednesday edition of *The Lennox Valley Hometown News*, "Missouri Flame Thrower Heats Up Valley," when she got the phone call from Vera Penrod, chair of the Lennox Valley Auburn Hat Society.

"I suppose you've heard the news," began Vera, "but I felt it my civic duty to make sure you, as editor of our town's newspaper, got the information from a reliable source. I knew you would want to get a first-hand account right away."

Iris was no stranger to Vera's "civic-mindedness" and could only imagine whether there had been another breach in protocol at the weekly Farmer's Market or perhaps if Father O'Reilly was drinking a Miller Lite at the Hoffbrau again. Iris could fill a book with the many acts of self-proclaimed "civic duty" carried about by Vera Penrod through the years.

This call was different, however. For once, Vera, just off the phone with Diane Curtis, had something newsworthy.

Timing is everything, not just in the news business, but in most of life. If Reverend Whedbee, superintendent of the Spring County District of the Methodist Church, had just waited one more day to make the announcement about Sarah Hyden-Smith's appointment, it would have been too late for the story to make the front page of *The Lennox Valley Hometown News.*

Vera couldn't wait to share what she had learned. It was just the type of information a woman of her stature would own.

"Diane Curtis," she began, "is chair of the Methodist Church Pastor-Parish Committee. That's their group for hiring a minister."

Vera could hardly contain herself. Iris was well familiar with how Methodists appointed their ministers and with the role of the PPR committee, but Penrod acted as if it was all brand new to the seasoned journalist.

"She just received the call and learned the new pastor is going to be a woman," Vera almost squealed into the phone. She let the news sink in before adding, "Have you ever heard of such a thing?"

When the phone rang, with Vera on the other end, Iris was laying out the headline for what she thought would be her next front-page story. Iris stopped cold as Vera shared the news.

A new preacher at the Methodist Church wouldn't normally be

front-page news. Methodists tend to change preachers almost as often as underwear. But a woman minister? In Lennox Valley? This was most certainly front-page news.

Iris slyly grinned as she imagined the impact of the story. The timing was less than perfect. A good portion of the town would learn of the news first on *Renderings with Raymond*. Sure, the explosion of letters to the editor would make her work that much easier in the coming weeks, but Iris wanted to be the first to break the story.

Iris made a monumental decision. She called Scott Critchlow, owner of the printing plant in Springfield, to ask if he could print *The Hometown News* overnight instead of waiting until Tuesday afternoon, when he normally printed the paper.

Wanting to keep his longtime customer happy, Critchlow agreed, and Iris was going to have a special edition on the street Tuesday morning, just in time to beat Raymond Cooper, of *Renderings with Raymond* fame, to the story.

She had to work fast. She called her lone reporter, a young intern from the local junior college, and told him to interview Reverend Billy Joe Prather of First Baptist Church and Father O'Reilly to get their opinions concerning the breaking news while she finished the rest of the paper.

In small-town papers in 1998, it was still common to prepare the pages on boards, with stories and headlines waxed on to create the pages. Photos were handled separately, then spliced into the film from which the printing plates were made. It would take a herculean effort to prepare the new front page, finish the other pages and get the pages and pictures to the printer by 9:00 p.m.

The front page headline, in 120-point type, read: "Turn Up the Volume for New Methodist Pastor." Just underneath was the subhead, "Move Over, Missouri Flame Thrower, and Make Room."

As Iris finished pasting on the headline, she stood back and looked at the finished page, minus the pictures, of course.

"Oh, my," she said to herself. "This is going to be the biggest story in years."

Chapter Ten

Raymond Cooper
Town counselor

Her intentions were innocent enough as Juliette Stoughton purchased her very first copy of *The Lennox Valley Hometown News* on Tuesday, May 5, 1998. She had read the newspaper once before upon finding an old copy under a phone book at the home where she and her "soulmate" lived together before he found another soulmate and moved on. Now, stranded on her own in a place with no friends and no obvious place to make friends, Juliette made her first trip alone to the town square.

Juliette was unaware that the town's newspaper normally came out on Wednesday mornings. The upcoming arrival of Sarah Hyden-Smith would soon affect more than the newspaper schedule.

Little did the good folks of The Valley know on Monday evening, as they watched *Walker, Texas Ranger* and reruns of *Murder, She Wrote*, the very foundation of their community was shaking with the first whispers of Hyden-Smith's appointment.

The reaction to Long's front page headline, "Turn up the Volume for New Methodist Pastor," was swift. First Baptist Church pastor Billy Joe Prather's call surprised Father O'Reilly of All Saints Catholic Church.

"Have you read it yet?" bellowed Reverend Prather. "A woman preacher?" he shouted louder. "What is the world coming to?"

"Just now," answered "the good father," as Vera Penrod liked to call him. "I certainly didn't see this coming. But I suppose it was bound to happen, sooner or later."

Both religious leaders were surprised when they were contacted by Long's only reporter, Boyd Sanders, around 9:00 p.m. the night before. Boyd, a local junior college student, could barely gather the nerve to call the shepherds of the town's largest flocks, but he did as instructed. Seeing the news in print, however, made it seem all the more real.

Prather made some comments about Biblical literacy and a woman's place. Father O'Reilly was a bit more diplomatic, but he expressed his surprise at the selection. Neither mentioned the possibility of a piano-playing spouse to the reporter.

The strongest reaction, however, came from Raymond Cooper, host of *Renderings with Raymond*. Iris Long's plan to get the paper on the streets of Lennox Valley before his Tuesday show worked to perfection, and Raymond was livid. Cooper did not like the idea of Long beating him to a story. He had been beyond excited at the prospect of breaking the news first on his Tuesday show at noon. He had been outsmarted by Long once again, and his response would be harsh and swift.

It's important to know that Raymond could not have cared less about the new Methodist pastor. Woman pastor or man pastor, it made no difference to him. He hadn't graced the entryway of a church, other than to attend a few weddings and funerals, in 50 years. That would change, however, as he quietly prepared his secret plans to make a run for the mayor's office in the upcoming November election.

Raymond realized it would soon be important that he be an active church member. No self-respecting politician had a chance of winning a public office in our town without the support of the church-going folks. For now, however, he was much less interested in church news than the fact Iris Long's headline reached the eyes of most Valley residents before his show hit the air. Iris had a habit of foiling his best laid plans, and she wasn't going to get away with it this time. Raymond, you see, always had a plan.

Unwilling to let the community think he had been outsmarted by Iris again, Raymond developed a strategy to turn his defeat into victory. As was often the case, he planned his words carefully in advance. His audience was larger than usual as more than 700 good folks of The Valley tuned in to hear his reaction to the announcement. Let's face it, this was the biggest news to hit The Valley in decades, and everybody wanted in on the discussion.

Before taking calls, Raymond explained that he had a few words for the listening audience.

"Yes, friends," began Raymond, "I read this morning's headline in the so-called '*Hometown News*'." Then, after a dramatic pause, he continued. "Of course, I received this information in plenty of time to break the story, but I decided it would be prudent to give the good folks at the Methodist Church time to make their own announcement before spreading this information among the community like a small-minded gossip."

You could feel the warmth growing among the audience, knowing their on-air champion was once again looking after their best interests. It was just like him, they thought, to seek the well-being of his listeners rather than rushing to gain glory for himself.

Raymond had much of our town fooled. His faithful would believe anything he told them.

Rather than "besmirching whatever dignity the Methodist Church can muster after the local paper's unfortunate decision," Raymond informed the listeners he had other, more important, issues to discuss. Opening the phone lines so listeners could call in, Raymond asked his audience to share any thoughts they had concerning Iris Long's alleged connections to the Federal Reserve System or any increases they had noticed in egg prices.

Marvin Walsh was the first to chime in. Elbert Lee Jones was next. Thinking back, it was amazing to think two local dairy farmers cared so much about the federal government.

In 1998, however, anything was possible in my hometown.

Chapter Eleven

Perry Prince
One fine grocer

Perry Prince was the kind of man everyone would want living in their hometown. As owner of Valley Country Store, Perry was a friend to just about everyone in The Valley.

With the closest real supermarket 16 miles away in Springfield, the good folks of Lennox Valley relied on Perry for their everyday goods like fruit, dairy products and Jell-O. It was comforting to know the dietary needs of The Valley were in good hands. Perry had inherited the business from his father, who had it passed to him from his father, the founder.

Perry was more than a grocer. He was friendly. He was fair. He never tried to get rich off his neighbors. Like his father, Perry worked to make an honest living.

While a pound of apples in Springfield supermarkets cost 99 cents per pound, Perry sold better quality apples for 79 cents per pound. When asked, he'd say, "You wouldn't believe how much they mark up their produce."

It wasn't unusual for Perry to toss an apple to an entering customer, "On the house."

His honesty was a major reason people felt they could trust him. As he rang up their groceries, Perry would listen to their woes, from stories of sick children, to dying parents, to problems with the harvest. He heard it all.

One of Perry's funniest memories was listening to the three protestant ministers discuss a recent Valley-wide revival. Father O'Reilly and his flock at All Saints didn't go in for such things, but the other three churches on the square held a revival meeting together every four years. These were held on odd years, so there would be no competition with the Summer Olympics. For church-goers, these revivals were bigger than the Olympics.

Pastors in small towns can't help but run into each other in public places. Their meeting at the Perry's store wasn't planned in advance. It just happened. Thankfully, it offered entertainment for Perry on an otherwise slow night.

"Brother Svendsen," Billy Joe Prather, pastor at First Baptist Church, asked the Lutheran pastor, "how were your results from the revival?"

Svendsen, senior pastor of the church, paused thoughtfully before answering, "They were wonderful."

Lutherans were used to adding new Valley residents to their rolls now and then, but it was a nice surprise to get converts coming from other Lennox Valley congregations.

"We added three souls to our flock," he beamed. "How did your congregation do, Brother Prather?"

Billy Joe did his best to appear humble, but he couldn't hold back his feelings as he grinned from ear to ear. "Oh, we had a wonderful revival. One of the best ever. Six souls found their way to our congregation."

"That's truly wonderful," responded Pastor Svendsen, a bit envious.

Turning to Reverend Vickers, Brother Prather asked, "And how about the Methodists?"

Perry still laughs when he remembers the Methodist pastor's response: "We had a better week than either of you."

Obviously surprised, Billy Joe asked, "Really, how many souls were added to your church?"

Reverend Vickers had their attention, then continued. "Oh, we didn't add any souls, but we got rid of our nine biggest trouble makers."

The Lutheran and Baptist ministers seemed to miss the humor, but Perry couldn't help but chuckle to himself.

Since venturing alone to town for the first time a week earlier, Juliette Stoughton had visited Valley Country Store twice to buy groceries. As a vegetarian, she found Perry's store was the perfect place to get the fruits, vegetables, and legumes on which she survived.

By now, Juliette and Perry were on a first-name basis, and for the first time, Juliette brought up a topic that didn't include produce. "Perry, may I ask you something?"

"Well, sure," he answered.

Juliette hesitated for a moment before asking, "Do you take part in the annual turkey shoot at the Baptist Church?"

Little did Perry know the First Baptist Church Annual Men's Breakfast and Turkey Shoot had been about the only thing on Juliette's mind for weeks, other than her soulmate, Chris Roadhouse, who had left her for a girl in Springfield months earlier.

Perry explained, as the only grocer in town, he wasn't free to attend the breakfast or the turkey shoot. He was needed at the store. So what he knew of it, he learned from reading *The Hometown News* or hearing winning shooters brag about their victories in his store.

"I see," she said, without asking more.

She left Prince's wondering if Perry was opposed to the idea of shooting turkeys at the church or if, as may have been the case, he was just too busy to attend. He didn't seem like the type who would kill unsuspecting creatures. She wished she had asked. For now, though, Perry Prince was still on Juliette's "good" list.

Juliette hadn't met many folks in The Valley, so neither her good list nor bad list was very long. But she felt it necessary to maintain mental lists, often recording notes on sticky-pads she kept on her dinner table. Generally, they ended up on her refrigerator door.

As she entered her home, Juliette could hear *Renderings with Raymond* on the radio. The host was going on about egg prices and said something about the newspaper editor's connections to inflation. At first, she thought she was hearing things, but she soon learned he was actually going on about egg prices. She quickly turned it off.

As she sat at her dining table, she jotted two notes and stuck them on the refrigerator door:

"Good list:
Perry Prince"

and

"Bad list:
Raymond Cooper"

Chapter Twelve

Raymond Cooper
He's our man!

In June 1998, the mayor of my hometown was none other than "Silver Tongue" Dick Bland. When he first ran for mayor in 1994, his campaign slogan was "Everybody's Friend," and that seemed like a pretty good description of our leader.

"Silver Tongue," as just about everyone called him, did pretty well as mayor. Sure, there were a few folks who got on the wrong side of Bland over the years, but overall he was loved by just about everybody.

I suppose I should have said he was loved by just about everybody before 1998. That's when Raymond Cooper started taking shots at the mayor on his daily *Renderings with Raymond* radio show.

Though his listening audience wasn't aware, Cooper had firmly set his sights on the mayor's seat, and that meant Dick Bland needed to get out of the way. It's amazing how a nice guy like Dick Bland could be made out to be a scoundrel through the power of the airwaves, but that's exactly what happened to "Silver Tongue."

Iris Long, editor of *The Lennox Valley Hometown News*, was no fan of Raymond and could see he was using his radio show to cause tension among the good folks of The Valley. So on June 3, 1998, Long published an interview with Dick Bland titled:

"Silver Tongue" Debunks Cooper's Tomfoolery

In the interview, Mayor Bland fielded several questions about the Federal Reserve System. Long's favorite quote was, "I have never been approached or contacted by the Federal Reserve System, though I would gladly lend my expertise if asked."

Several good folks of The Valley giggled as they read about their mayor offering his assistance to the "feds." Like many small-town mayors, it was all Bland could do to stay on top of local issues.

The mayor went on to describe the "outlandish" idea that egg prices had anything to do with the federal government. He noted that a dozen eggs were selling at the Country Store for $1.09. He went on to share in 1992, eggs sold for 94 cents. That, he told Long, was a 16 percent rise in six years, while inflation over that same period was 17 percent.

If the Federal Reserve System was inflating egg prices over that period, it seemed to "Silver Tongue" the price would be significantly higher than $1.09.

"If anything," he continued, "the feds have been holding the price of a dozen eggs below the inflation rate."

They didn't call Mayor Bland "Silver Tongue" for nothing. He knew how to drive a point home. And, for once, it was a valid point. Eggs had actually increased in price less than the cost of inflation over the previous six years. If the Federal Reserve System was purposely inflating the price of eggs, they would surely outpace the rate of inflation.

Anyone reading the June 3 edition of *The Hometown News* would think Dick Bland had hit a home run, knocking the negative murmurings of Raymond Cooper right out of the park. Little did "Silver Tongue" or Iris Long realize they had played right into Cooper's hands.

"Friends," began Raymond on his Wednesday show, "I feel as though my reputation has been assassinated in today's so-called 'Hometown News'."

Bland didn't have the only "Silver Tongue" in town. Raymond Cooper knew listeners would subliminally associate "assassinate" with politics.

"What did I do to deserve this type of attack?" asked Cooper. "You would think our mayor and chief news informer would have more important things to do than besmirch my reputation," he said. "Why are they so worried about me? I'm just one citizen trying to speak out against injustice."

The first caller, Elbert Lee Jones, was furious the local "rag" would attack a champion of the people like Raymond Cooper. He called for the mayor's and the editor's immediate resignations.

Cooper was quick to remind his caller that the mayor had a right to his opinion, no doubt influenced by some connection with the Federal Reserve System. And expecting Bland to resign wasn't realistic, as a new election was being held in just five months.

"Maybe," accelerated Raymond in a calm, firm voice, "someone will rise up to speak for the people in the upcoming election," although he admitted having no idea who that person would be.

"I nominate you!" blurted the next caller, Earl Goodman. "You are the leader we need."

Goodman delivered the mail in Lennox Valley, making him the only federal employee in town. For a lot of folks, his opinion carried a lot of weight.

"That's flattering," Cooper said, "but I've never given political office a moment's thought," lying through his teeth. "I'm sure there's a more worthy candidate out there."

The next caller, Marvin Walsh, was even more intense. "I second Earl's nomination!"

Cooper, feigning meekness, was silent for a moment, rare for

Raymond, before responding in a soft, firm voice, "I just don't know. I somehow feel it's more important for me to be a watchdog, keeping our government in check."

Callers would have none of that.

"Mayor Cooper," Thelma Biggers almost shouted into her phone, no doubt partially a result of her hearing loss, "we need you to be our mayor. Not that silver-tongued Devil!"

"Wow," answered Raymond. "I had no idea the citizens of this community felt so strongly about this."

Cooper paused dramatically, letting the tension increase. Raymond knew how to create the perfect atmosphere to stir listeners.

"If my town needs me," Cooper shouted, "how can I turn away?"

Who would have thought not one Valley resident would call in about the new Methodist preacher on June 3? Raymond had once again proven effective at turning emotions in his favor.

It was finally summer, and things were really heating up among the good folks of Lennox Valley.

Chapter Thirteen

Lady Preacher

Sarah Hyden-Smith arrives for a visit

It had been almost three months since the members of Lennox Valley Methodist Church learned their pastor, Reverend Glynn Vickers, was being moved in June, and it had been four weeks since that fateful moment on May 4 when Diane Curtis, chair of the Methodist Church Pastor-Parish Committee, received the call from the Springfield district superintendent to inform her that Sarah Hyden-Smith was being appointed as the new minister in Lennox Valley.

It's funny how something can seem so important at one moment, then be almost forgotten the next. That's kind of how it was with the news of Reverend Hyden-Smith. When word first broke out Lennox Valley was about to get its first clergywoman, the news was so hot Iris Long published *The Hometown News* a day early. That was something that hadn't been done since August 16, 1977, when Elvis Presley died.

During my growing-up years, I was often reminded there is one thing that trumps just about everything else in small towns: politics. And the good folks of Lennox Valley had just been surprised by the biggest political announcement since Helen Walker decided to run against her husband, Mayor Jay Walker, in his bid for reelection in November 1976.

Just three days earlier, on June 3, during the Wednesday edition of *Renderings with Raymond*, the audience was divided between shocked and delighted to hear Raymond Cooper announce his "willingness" to acquiesce to the will of his listeners and run against "Silver Tongue" Dick Bland in the upcoming November election. Suddenly, news of a new woman minister took a back seat to the sizzling political announcement.

Just the same, Diane Curtis arranged a meeting of the Pastor-Parish Committee at 4:30 Saturday afternoon. Originally, word of the meeting was the talk of the town as Methodists and others who weren't even members of the committee called Diane to ask if they could attend.

Some had heard stories of a female Pentecostal minister in the 1930s who came through town as part of a "Holy Ghost Revival." The evangelist, it was told, dressed in a police uniform, sat in the saddle of a police motorcycle and blew the siren over and over.

Next, old-timers like to reminisce, she drove the motorcycle, with its deafening roar, across the access ramp to the pulpit, slammed on the brakes, then raised a white-gloved hand to shout, "Stop! You're speeding to Hell!"

Sixty years had passed since the "Holy Roller Traffic Cop" came through town, and the idea of an honest-to-goodness woman pastor living right here in Lennox Valley was more than many folks could imagine.

"Do you think," folks would ask, "she will ride a motorcycle up on the altar of the church?"

Most folks knew a motorcycle-riding minister was unlikely. Still, non-Methodists privately joked about a woman minister in Lennox Valley, while Methodists nervously waited to see their new pastor and learn for themselves what they were in for.

So it was that Sarah Hyden-Smith innocently pulled into a

parking space at the Methodist Church, expecting cake, punch and a lovely meeting with her new flock. She guessed they would probably meet around a Sunday school class table. Methodists are big on Sunday school, actually creating the concept as a way to educate children at a time when the England government wasn't too favorable about the idea.

Diane Curtis, who had been watching through the window of the fellowship hall, rushed out to welcome Sarah to her new church. Diane seemed friendly enough to the new pastor, albeit a bit nervous. Curtis looked in Sarah's car for a husband, but didn't see one.

"He probably stayed home," she thought, "so Sarah can focus on her new flock."

Expecting the usual six or seven members who normally make up a Pastor-Parish Committee, Hyden-Smith was quite surprised to walk into a room with more than 80 folks seated in six rows across the fellowship hall.

It was like a "who's who" of Lennox Valley. Local celebrities including Dick Bland and Vera Penrod were present. Many of the town's prominent business owners, including Farley Puckett, owner of the hardware store, were on hand. Marvin Walsh and Elbert lee Jones, local farmers and friends of Raymond Cooper, were seated in the second row.

Interestingly, Cooper himself wasn't anywhere to be seen. He had mentioned he didn't want to create a spectacle of the situation at the Methodist church. Maybe he meant it. After all, he couldn't be as bad as Iris Long seemed to think.

Following a brief introduction by Diane Curtis, Sarah told the group she was thrilled to be appointed to Lennox Valley and asked the eerily silent audience if they had any questions or thoughts they would like to ask or share.

Looking back, I'm not sure why anyone was surprised when Elbert Lee Jones raised his hand and asked, "What's your stand on the Federal Reserve System?"

Back at the radio station, Raymond Cooper leaned back in his chair, grinning an almost evil grin, as he imagined what was taking place at the Methodist church at that very moment.

Chapter Fourteen

QVC Reigns

TV addiction can be problematic

With all the craziness surrounding Raymond Cooper's candidacy for mayor and the appointment of Sarah Hyden-Smith to the Methodist Church, it would be easy to get the idea that life was never normal in my hometown. Let me make something clear: I'm sure there were normal days during my teen years.

It's just that I don't remember any of them.

As I think back, 1998 was clearly different from the times we currently live in. There were no cellphones, iPads or texting. While our parents were watching *Saving Private Ryan* at the theaters, we were home playing *Super Mario Brothers* and *Legend of Zelda*.

In 1998, we liked to think that men were men and women were women. Men, when not annihilating paper plates at the annual First Baptist Church turkey shoot, spent much of their time discussing sports or playing dominoes. These discussions often took place at the VFW post or Ruritan Club.

Women, however, had found a much more addictive pastime by the late 1990s. When it first appeared on the TV screen ten or so years earlier, QVC shopping network took the women of Lennox

55

Valley by storm. Indeed, women in small towns throughout America seemed enchanted by the glow of the screen, and more than one battle erupted following the arrival of a CD by Italian pop artist Giovanni, which sold more than 100,000 copies during a two-hour sales pitch on QVC in the midst of a cold stretch of weather one February.

I'm guessing at least 300 of those CDs arrived in Lennox Valley mailboxes. Only Earl Goodman, town mailman, would know for sure.

You name it and you could buy it on QVC. Jewelry, music, wedding dresses and makeup were all available with a quick call to an 800 number. Payment was no problem because viewers were reminded they could pay for their purchase in "two easy payments."

Lisa Robertson, a former beauty queen from Tennessee, was the favorite QVC host among Lennox Valley viewers. Watching Lisa each day was like spending time with your beautiful, 33-year-old, best friend. Women from small towns like Lennox Valley would call in and talk with Lisa, who would give them personal advice on air, much like any best friend.

Discussing a recent purchase of a "Hugs and Kisses" bracelet by Cheryl, from Hanover, Pennsylvania, Lisa was quick to point out, "Your mom is so lucky. I don't think you could do any better, Cheryl," with a loving smile.

I'm certain Cheryl beamed as she presented that bracelet to her mother just "three to five business days" later. Of course, as excited as she was, she probably kicked in the extra $12.95 for rush shipping.

It's hard to know for sure, but rumor has it the FedEx box containing the Sandglass alarm clock was the final straw for T.J. Bordewyck. It wasn't so much that his wife, Sherilyn, had purchased her third alarm clock that year as it was seeing the red and blue overnight label and knowing she had authorized a $12.95 surcharge to keep from waiting three to five restless days for her latest purchase to arrive.

T.J. was livid as he burst out the door and made his way to the town square, where only the Hoffbrau and the Country Store were open. Figuring that coming back home with the smell of Miller Lite on his breath might not be the best idea, T.J. opted for a "cool down period" at the store.

The good folks of The Valley could count on Perry Prince for a smile and a listening ear, and so it was at 7:10 p.m. on June 11, 1998, T.J. made his way into Prince's.

"You're open late tonight, Perry," T.J. bellowed as he walked to the counter. "I figured you'd be closed by now."

"Yes," responded Perry, "I'm gathering some things together to take to Hubert Parkins."

"Is something wrong?" asked T.J. "You don't usually make deliveries."

Perry was surprised T.J. hadn't heard the news. "You must not have heard. Deloris passed away this afternoon," he said with obvious sadness. "They've been married 64 years. It's hard to believe."

He asked T.J. if there was something he could do for him.

After a few moments of deep contemplation, T.J. murmured, "I was hoping you might have some flowers."

Entering his home with a bouquet of yellow daffodils for Sherilyn, T.J. asked, "Where's that new clock? I was thinking it would look nice on our mantle."

Kevin Slimp's

The Good Folks of Lennox Valley

Shocking News!
Valley Methodists are in for a surprise

As April moved aside for May 1998, the good folks of Lennox Valley had no idea how their world was about to change on Monday, May 4.

On Talk Radio 880's "Rendering With Raymond," callers were equally divided between two topics of vital importance.

The first had to do with a book coming to America that was all the rage among teens in Europe.

"Harry Potter," barked the first caller, Martha Jean Bratton, was "of the devil" and "has no place in the hands of any self-respecting young person."

Host Raymond Cooper felt certain, he told his listeners, that enthusiasm for this "Potter character" would wane soon enough. "I doubt it will even make it to an American bookshelf," he quipped.

Raymond felt less confident concerning discussion revolving around the Federal Reserve System, which took up much of the next three hours. Raymond was sure "insiders," like Iris Long, were fanning the flames in support of the government. Raymond noted, with a sly grin not seen by his listeners, that the Hofbrau had raised the price of a Denver omelette from $3.25 to $3.29 over the weekend, more proof of the havoc resulting from federal mismanagement.

The big news of May 4 didn't happen until 3:10, just after the show went off the air. That was when Diane Curtis, chair of the Lennox Valley Methodist Church Pastor/Parish Committee, received a call from Rev. James Whedbee, Springfield district superintendent.

Methodists, you see, don't select their own ministers like most Protestant churches. Their pastors are assigned by bishops and word is sent to the individual congregations through district superintendents.

"Mrs. Curtis," began the soft-voiced superintendent, "I'm calling with good news. After prayerful consideration, we have selected a new pastor for Lennox Valley."

Diane had been on pins and needles for weeks, wondering who the new pastor would be. Like everyone else at the Methodist Church, she hoped for a powerful orator, with a strong singing voice and, if the Lord felt especially gracious, a wife who played piano.

Reverend Vickers had been very popular during his three years, but in a congregation as small as Lennox Valley, three years was about as long as ministers stayed before they were sent to a larger congregation or retired.

"The Reverend Sarah Hyden-Smith is being appointed to Lennox Valley," Reverend Whedbee uttered before continuing, "and her first Sunday will be June 14."

There was a long pause before Diane responded, "Did you say 'Sarah?'"

The district superintendent mentioned that Diane's committee should start making plans to welcome the new pastor.

"Perhaps a potluck meal after her first service," he suggested tacitly. "Some music might be nice. Maybe someone could play piano," he added.

Wisely, Diane held back from responding with her first instinct, "I'm guessing the new pastor's wife doesn't play piano." Instead, she replied, "Yes, I suppose we should."

As Diane Curtis, hung up the phone, Iris Long, editor of *The Lennox Valley Hometown News*, penned what she thought would be her next front page story. Like much in Lennox Valley, that was about to change.

Lennox Valley: The Book will be available from Amazon, Barnes & Noble and other fine bookstores beginning June 1, 2017.

READ MORE @ LENNOXVALLEY.COM

latest contro... nately for him, this created even more interest in his daily show, "Renderings With Raymond."

As it came to pass, Independence Day landed on Sunday in 1998, and the members of First Baptist Church were vocal in their insistence that a fireworks spectacle should not be competing with their devotion to The Almighty on The Lord's Day.

Catholics, Lutherans and Methodists didn't seem too concerned with the potential competition for the Lord's attention. There were a couple of reasons for this.

First, the Baptists were the only group to hold services on Sunday night, so non-Baptist folks of the Valley were free to enjoy their evenings as they

realized tha... with an important issue if he was going to be elected mayor of Lennox Valley: Where to go to church.

You see, while Cooper enjoyed a large listening audience each day, he knew that he was going up against "Silver Tongue" Dick Bland in the August election, and as a member of First Baptist Church, Bland has at least a couple of hundred votes in his pocket, maybe more.

Raymond realized that, for most folks, it would be hard to vote against someone they sat near in church every Sunday. And since he hadn't attended church since he was a young boy, Raymond had no built-in church constituency.

The Meth... possibility, but Raymond was concerned that he would lose votes if he attended a church with a female pastor.

The clear choice, it seemed, was Lennox Valley Lutheran Church. They wouldn't insist that he be baptized, since he had been sprinkled as a baby, and he had heard that an "invitation" was offered at the end of the contemporary service, led by Brother Jacob, every Sunday morning.

His timing and performance would be critical. Raymond would need more Hoffbrau receipts as he devised his strategy for Independence Day, 1998.

READ MORE @ LENNOXVALLEY.COM

58

Chapter Fifteen

The Prettiest Girl
Mary Ann Tinkersley

Mary Ann Tinkersley was the prettiest girl in all of Lennox Valley during my teenage years, and truth be told, she was the primary reason for the drop in my algebra scores between the winter and spring semesters of 1998.

My mother insisted I spend at least 60 minutes each night studying algebra. What she didn't understand was Mary Ann sat one row to my left and one seat ahead of me in class, and no amount of studying was going to make up for the confusion she stirred in my brain cells each day from 1:15 to 2:05.

Lennox Valley wasn't big enough for our own high school, so Mary Ann and I both attended school 11 miles away at Central Valley High School. CVHS was born through a merger of West Central High School and Lennox Valley High School back in the 1950s. It comprised a mix of kids from Lennox Valley and the area west of Springfield, the county seat.

Located between the two towns, though a little closer to Springfield, CVHS was the birthplace of my imagined romance with Mary Ann.

During my sophomore year, there were 103 students from

Lennox Valley at Central, meaning most of us had grown up together and knew each other pretty well. Mary Ann and I had been close friends in elementary school, but as is often the case, we parted ways as we grew into adolescence.

In towns like Lennox Valley, it's common practice for high school students to raise livestock during the school year and through the summer in anticipation of the FFA judging at the August county fair. The FFA judging is a big deal in a place like The Valley, and most teenagers participated in one event or another.

As it happened in 1998, both Mary Ann and I were raising lambs. Lambs weren't the easiest animals to raise. A lot of my friends entered rabbits, thinking they would be the easiest to care for. I chose a lamb because my father convinced me I would be taking the easy way out with a rabbit. It was hard to win a livestock argument with my dad.

It's a big deal to raise a prize-winning animal, so teenagers went all out to get their livestock in the best condition possible. Beginning in March, when the weather was more supportive, I would walk my lamb, Archibald, every evening just before supper, usually for 10 minutes.

Imagine my surprise when, on June 4, 1998, I came upon Mary Ann walking her lamb, Snowflake, one block from the town square, just around the corner from All Saints Church. Pretty soon, our "accidental" meetings took place every night at that same corner.

Ten minutes became fifteen minutes, and before long, we had the healthiest lambs in all Spring County.

As we walked, we'd help each other prepare for the livestock judging and the "oral reasons" section of the judging. Oral reasons is a process dreamed up by cruel farmers in decades past who obviously enjoyed watching future farmers forced to participate in their greatest fear, public speaking.

Basically, the idea was that we would judge livestock raised by other future farmers against the "ideal" animal. Not only did we have to group the unknowing contestants into categories, but we had to give oral explanations of why we placed each animal where we did. In short, it was worse than algebra.

Most of our walks were peaceful. A few times, I took Mary Ann by Perry's store and bought a Mountain Dew to quench her thirst.

We would often walk an extra block to see the latest sign at First Baptist Church. Loren, who changed the sign almost daily, would sometimes misspell or misuse a word, and we'd enjoy the anticipation of his latest literary creation glowing as dusk settled in.

Now and then we would encounter something memorable while walking our lambs, like the night we saw T.J. Bordewyck slam his door and zip toward the town square, murmuring under his breath about overnight shipping. T.J. was a nice man, but it was rumored that he had a pretty bad temper sometimes. We'd never seen it, but he didn't seem too happy that night.

We would hear arguments from time to time while passing homes. More than once, we heard Sarah Goolsby arguing with her parents over her refusal to eat the "animal carcass" that her mother had prepared for dinner. Her mother didn't seem too thrilled with her daughter's eating habits.

Most disagreements seemed to be over the Federal Reserve System. In retrospect, it's amazing how upset people could get over a government agency. More than once, we heard folks say some pretty harsh words about Iris Long and her government connections.

We would also hear people discussing the new preacher at the Methodist Church. Some seemed upset the Methodists would appoint a woman to Lennox Valley.

Funny, though, 15-year-olds don't concern themselves with things like the Federal Reserve or Methodist pastors while walking their lambs through the town square near the end of the day.

There were more important things to think about. Things like the upcoming livestock judging or the class schedule for our junior year.

Yes, Mary Ann Tinkersley was the prettiest girl in Lennox Valley, and I was walking with her. The Federal Reserve System couldn't do anything to mess that up.

Chapter Sixteen

Rumor Has It
By Maxine Miller

It didn't take a Nielsen rating to uncover the favorite local entertainment in Lennox Valley in 1998. Without our own TV station, newspaper and radio were our outlets for local news. Our paper came out every Wednesday morning like clockwork. A group of retired townspeople could be seen sipping coffee at the Dairy Queen on State Highway 11, beginning around 6:30 a.m. each week, while they waited for the paper to arrive.

Everyone's most anticipated column was "Rumor Has It" by Maxine Miller. This is where we would get the news that wouldn't quite make it in one of Iris Long's more, shall we say, journalistic columns. As you might guess, Maxine's favorite phrase was "rumor has it," and each of her columns began with those words.

"Rumor has it," she would begin, "T.J. Bordewyck was seen arriving home late in the evening on June 11, carrying a bouquet of flowers from Prince's Country Store."

From that point, Maxine would elaborate on the reasons a man might bring flowers to his wife so late in the evening and why, with all the flowers in the world, he would choose to bring daffodils.

"As I remember," Maxine wrote, "Sherilyn and T.J. were married in the fall, so those weren't anniversary flowers."

"If it was her birthday," Maxine penned, "perhaps he should have thought ahead and ordered something nice from QVC."

Maxine loved to stir up the dust, and Lennox Valley was one dusty place. Maxine used to write, "The nice thing about living in a small town is when you don't know what you are doing, somebody else does."

It seemed like most gossip in Lennox Valley was born in one of three places: Maxine's weekly column, Raymond Cooper's radio show, or Caroline's Beauty Salon. To be sure, however, Caroline had enough problems of her own after marrying her high school sweetheart, Walter Bittle, in 1989.

Walter, it seems, was quite the physical specimen in high school and was one of Lennox Valley's most decorated athletes. In 1989, Walter reached the state track and field finals for the third straight year. His specialty was the pole vault, which won him a gold medal at the state meet his senior year.

One can just imagine the teasing Caroline endured during high school while dating "Walter the Vaulter." Kids can be cruel, and Caroline was no stranger to cruelty. That's probably why Caroline tried to keep mean, spiteful gossip to a minimum as best she could. Plus, she had her own personal issues.

No one noticed when Walter left three weeks earlier. He took a garbage bag full of clothes, along with most of the money from the family bank account, and hadn't returned. This was no time for Caroline to be spreading rumors about anyone else.

The folks of Lennox Valley would figure out soon enough something was amiss in Caroline's life. She saw no need in sharing her problems with others. Not yet, anyway.

That wasn't the case with Maxine. Iris Long, editor of *Hometown News*, wasn't thrilled with many of the rumors she would spread, but Maxine was a big reason many of the good folks of The Valley read *The Hometown News* each week.

So it was on the week of Sarah Hyden-Smith's arrival to the Valley. Just four days before her first sermon at the Methodist church, Sarah opened the paper to read, "Rumor has it that the new minister at Lennox Valley Methodist Church is single."

Sarah was afraid to read further, but she had no choice.

"Fortunately," Maxine continued, "she won't be the only single pastor in Lennox Valley," referring to Brother Jacob at the Lutheran Church.

"I'm guessing," concluded Maxine, "that the Ministerial Alliance meetings are about to get much more interesting."

Maxine Miller had done it again.

The truth is, we didn't know if our new pastor was single or married. She might have been a widow, for all we knew. That wouldn't deter Maxine Miller, however. No blow was too low. Everyone was fair game, and she'd just taken her first shot at the town's newest resident.

Indeed, there was no shortage of entertainment in my hometown.

Chapter Seventeen

Sarah's First Sunday
Thank goodness for children

Sarah Hyden-Smith was usually a cheerful, confident woman. Lennox Valley Methodist Church was her second appointment, having served as an associate pastor at a larger church since graduating from a fine seminary in Central Ohio five years earlier.

Sarah, however, was no longer in Central Ohio, and today was a day of two firsts. It was the first time she stood in front of the congregation as "the pastor" and the first time she faced a congregation following a column in the local paper suggesting she and The Valley's other young pastor, Jacob Gehrig at Lennox Valley Lutheran Church, might create sparks not seen since the previous Fourth of July celebration.

The good Methodist folks of The Valley had burned the phone lines all week, sharing their thoughts concerning a supposedly single female with a hyphenated name. Was she divorced? A widow? Does she have a husband in some far off place, waiting to join her in their lovely village?

When she met with the parish committee a week earlier, she never mentioned her marital status. And since Elbert Lee Jones had used up his question when he asked about Sarah's stance on the

Federal Reserve System, there was no one left in the room with the courage to approach Sarah concerning the subject. Marvin Walsh thought about asking, but he was in a hurry to get to the VFW for the weekly domino tournament.

Her ring finger was conspicuously empty, and Sarah hadn't brought up the subject of a spouse, so everyone assumed she was single, or divorced, or a widow. And now that Maxine Miller had pretty much announced to the entire community in her column, "Rumor Has It," sparks might fly between the two young pastors in town, it was assumed by everyone Sarah Hyden-Smith was a single woman with a hyphenated name.

You would think adults would have learned their lesson about assuming, but assumptions are big things in small towns, and in more ways than one, Lennox Valley was very small.

It was appropriate the opening hymn, "O For a Thousand Tongues," was perhaps the all-time Methodist favorite. They love that song the way Lutherans love "A Mighty Fortress is Our God."

Sure, it may not carry the emotional baggage of the Baptist favorite, "Just As I Am," but there was no doubt you were in a Methodist church when the Charles Wesley favorite started ringing from the pipe organ.

"O for a thousand tongues to sing," the congregation roared. Methodists do love singing that hymn.

The next line of the hymn was a request for God to assist the singers in their proclamations.

Funny, Sarah was praying that same prayer as her congregation sang. "Gracious God," she prayed silently, "please assist me to proclaim."

As Sarah faced the congregation, her right hand shook a little as she placed it on the pulpit. No one noticed except Sarah. Her opening prayer seemed to go smoothly, and she could feel the congregation's eerie quietness as they seemingly waited for angels to appear or lightning to strike as the first female pastor in the history of Lennox Valley took the stage, ending the opening prayer with "Amen."

It was no coincidence, being the first Sunday with a new minister, coupled with that minister being a woman, the sanctuary of the old Methodist church was as full as it had been since a brief charismatic period following the release of *The Cross and the Switchblade* back in 1970.

Smiles filled the congregation as 22 children came forward for the children's sermon, which took place following the prayer. Sarah had been told that there were normally four or five children in attendance, so she was a surprised when she saw the throng approaching.

Sarah's plan was to have them each take a place along a rope, holding on as their pastor led them on a walk around the sanctuary. The idea behind the "rope walk" was that if anyone were to fall, someone would be right behind them to pick them up. Everything seemed to be going well as the new female pastor led the three- to eight-year-olds around the sanctuary, with smiling adults watching and listening as their children and grandchildren starred in the show. Sarah was surprised, however, as she led the parade back to the altar area, when she saw young Brad and Elizabeth Alwood sitting on the steps, just in front of the pulpit.

Sarah turned to Brad, the older of the two siblings, and innocently asked, "Why didn't you join us on our walk around the sanctuary?"

Brad's response brought down the house and guaranteed Sarah Hyden-Smith's first day as pastor was a success. "Because our daddy told us if we got up and walked around during children's sermon one more time, he was going to beat our butts."

No one remembered very much about Sarah's first sermon, but her first children's sermon was a huge success, and for the record, no one mentioned seeing angels or lightning at Lennox Valley

Methodist Church on that Sunday in the middle of June of 1998.

As with the arrival of any new pastor, a few Methodists secretly pined for the "good life" they had enjoyed, listening to Pastor Vickers pronounce his benediction, almost always with a quote from his favorite book (besides the Bible, of course), *Celebrity Quotes*. No one in the congregation was aware that the pastor's parting words each week were actually quotes from famous celebrities. Most just thought their shepherd had a gift usually reserved for poets and composers of ballads.

Some were as simple as, "And whichsoever way thou goest, may fortune follow," taken directly from *Journey to the Center of the Earth* by Jules Verne.

Other times, like when he borrowed a line written in 1954 by J.R.R. Tolkien, they were a bit more poetic: "Farewell, and may the blessing of Elves and Men and all Free Folk go with you. May the stars shine upon your faces."

Then, there were the benedictions that caused congregants to wonder if the good reverend had possibly stopped by the Hoffbrau for a Miller Lite – a habit generally frowned upon by many small town Methodists – while preparing for the next day's service. For example, he would sometimes use lines from popular songs of the 1960s: "As you part from this place, whisper words of wisdom." Then, instead of "Amen," he dismissed the congregation with, "Let it be."

The first time I remember hearing townsfolk whisper that it might be time for Pastor Vickers to consider retirement was after his most memorable benediction, in late 1997, "May the force be with you," to which they instinctively responded, "And also with you."

Was my hometown bizarre? Sometimes. Was it boring? Never. And as June ended, one citizen of The Valley was deep in contemplation, knowing this decision could determine if he would be the next mayor of our town.

Chapter Eighteen

I've Got the Spirit
Raymond Cooper finds religion

Truman Capote once wrote, "Fame is good for only one thing. They will cash your check in a small town."

Famous people weren't plentiful in my hometown as June moved into July of 1998, but we had one homegrown luminary, Raymond Cooper. Cooper had become our local celebrity, and he cherished the role.

Like most of the town, Raymond was engulfed in the latest controversy. Fortunately for him, this created even more interest in his daily radio show, *Renderings with Raymond*.

As it came to pass, Independence Day landed on Saturday in 1998, and the members of First Baptist Church were vocal in their insistence that members should not be staying up late and interfering with their devotion to The Almighty on The Lord's Day.

Catholics, Lutherans and Methodists didn't seem too concerned with the potential competition for the Lord's attention. There were a couple of reasons for this.

First, the Baptist church drew a lot more folks to their early service on Sunday, while most Methodists and Lutherans were sleeping in. There were a few hearty Catholics and contemporary Lutherans up early on Sunday, but the bulk of early risers were Baptists.

Secondly, most folks figured that God enjoyed a fireworks show as much as anyone else. While I was a child, there were many Fourth of July celebrations when I wondered what fireworks looked like from Heaven.

As important as the present quarrel was to Raymond's talk show, there was another matter vying for his attention. Though he'd rather put it off forever, Raymond realized that he had to deal with an important issue if he was going to be elected mayor of Lennox Valley: where to attend church.

You see, while Cooper enjoyed a large listening audience each day, he knew he was going up against "Silver Tongue" Dick Bland in the August election, and as a member of First Baptist Church, Bland had at least a couple of hundred votes in his pocket, maybe more.

Raymond realized, for most folks, it would be hard to vote against someone they sat near in church every Sunday. And since he hadn't attended church since he was a young boy, Raymond had no built-in church constituency.

Cooper carefully considered the pros and cons of each of the town's four congregations. He jotted his thoughts on the back of a Hoffbrau receipt as listeners called in to his show, howling about the failings of the Federal Reserve System or the audacity of shooting fireworks on the night before Sunday morning's worship.

All Saints Catholic Church was the first to be trimmed from the list. There were classes involved in joining the church, and that could take weeks.

First Baptist Church would be the obvious choice, if it wasn't for Dick Bland. They met three times every week, where they almost begged for folks to come down the aisle to join the church at the end of each service. But with Bland there, Cooper was unlikely to garner many new votes.

The Methodist Church was a possibility, but Raymond was concerned that he would lose votes if he attended a church with a female pastor.

The clear choice, it seemed, was Lennox Valley Lutheran Church. They wouldn't insist that he be baptized, since he had been sprinkled as a baby, and he had heard that an "invitation" was offered at the end of the contemporary service, led by Brother Jacob, every Sunday morning.

His timing and performance would be critical. It's hard to imagine it had been only 17 months since Raymond Cooper hatched his plan to use his celebrity to weasel his way into the mayor's seat in the upcoming election. With each passing day, listeners became more enraged at Raymond's favorite source of controversy, the dastardly actions of the Federal Reserve System. These actions, he claimed, were solely responsible for the soaring price of eggs.

The year 1998 was also eventful for Lennox Valley because it was just after Juliette Stoughton moved to town, although hardly anyone knew it at the time.

As one of only six vegetarians in all of The Valley, Juliette was chagrined by the thought of Baptist men traipsing around the church grounds, shooting innocent turkeys. The fact that women weren't invited made it that much worse.

Who knew that so many puzzle pieces would come together on one extraordinary day? It was on July 5 that both Juliette Stoughton and Raymond Cooper awoke, unbeknownst to each other, in their respective homes, earlier than usual for a Sunday morning. Both residents of The Valley were planning to attend church for the first time as adults, but for different reasons.

Juliette, still plotting her upcoming protest at First Baptist Church, had heard about the new pastor at Lennox Valley Methodist Church. In a moment of desperation, feeling the growing loneliness of a woman whose soulmate was gone for good, Juliette made the fateful decision to quietly slip in among the Methodists and see what this Sarah Hyden-Smith was all about. She was grasping for hope, and church seemed as good a place as any to find it.

Raymond's reason for attending church was a bit less noble. Coming to the conclusion he must be a faithful church member to win the upcoming election, he realized the clock was ticking and July 5 was to be the day he took the membership plunge. After much "prayerful thought," a phrase he would repeat often in the coming weeks, he selected the contemporary service at Lennox Valley Lutheran Church.

It would be a performance to be retold time and again over the coming years.

Raymond had been priming the pump all week on his daily radio show, *Renderings with Raymond*, as he prepared to carry out his evil scheme. Since Monday, talk had been rampant on the show concerning three topics:

• The Federal Reserve System, and Raymond's plan to address the problem by accepting his listeners' outcry to run for mayor in the upcoming election;

• The uproar by Billy Joe Prather, pastor of First Baptist Church, over the town's plans to shoot fireworks at 9:00 p.m. on July 4, potentially causing folks to skip the early worship;

• Raymond's constant reminder to his listeners that something was stirring within him, something so deep he couldn't put it into words.

In truth, something was stirring alright. Cooper's plan to join a church on July 5, in time to garner new votes in his election bid, was at hand.

His listeners were concerned. It wasn't like Raymond to have a problem putting anything into words. Could he be dying? Could he be in some sort of trouble? Could the Federal Reserve System be breathing down his throat? Listeners wanted to know. But if Raymond said he couldn't verbalize his inner murmurings, who were they to press their champion of the airwaves? He would, they trusted, explain in due time.

Raymond had a small problem as he prepared for his "religious awakening."

He was planning to attend Lennox Valley Lutheran Church, having found there was a "contemporary" service held in the Lutheran Fellowship Hall at 8:30 a.m. each week. The beauty of the contemporary service, Raymond learned, was Brother Jacob offered an invitation to join the church at the end of each service, something that wasn't done in the traditional service held upstairs in the sanctuary.

There was a slight problem. What Cooper knew about church invitations he learned during a brief period while attending a Pentecostal church with his grandmother almost 50 years earlier. Surely, he figured, things couldn't have changed that much.

When Sunday came, Raymond made his way into the Fellowship Hall at precisely 8:28 a.m. Fortunately, the fireworks didn't keep him from making it to the contemporary service. He quickly found a place in a folding metal chair in the back row. It seemed that the previous evening's fireworks display had kept some folks at home, and the smaller-than-usual crowd of only 13 worshipers was quick to notice a celebrity was in their midst. Such an appearance had never happened before at the contemporary service.

The Lutheran Church, he learned quickly after taking his seat in a folding metal chair, was a bit different than the Pentecostal church he remembered from his childhood. The songs were similar, though slightly less energetic. It was a contemporary service, after all. There was no speaking in tongues nor loud "Amens" as the minister spoke. Nonetheless, Cooper decided to stick with his plan.

Brother Jacob offered an invitation to join the church as the keyboard began playing "Lord of the Dance." Imagine everyone's surprise as Raymond ran down the center aisle, waving his arms and falling on the floor in front of Brother Jacob, in an attempt at being "slain in the spirit." If he remembered one thing from his

Pentecostal upbringing, it was that falling to the floor in religious ecstasy was expected during any authentic conversion.

Eventually, Cooper made his way to his feet as the congregation and Brother Jacob watched in horror.

"I'm ready to join," he told his new pastor.

That afternoon, as the good folks of Lennox Valley made their preparations for the continued Independence Day celebrations, word about the first "conversion" during a contemporary service spread like wildfire among the community. Could it be? Raymond Cooper? A Lutheran?

Iris Long, editor of *The Lennox Valley Hometown News*, initially heard about the miraculous event from Vera Penrod, president of the Auburn Hat Society.

"They said Raymond Cooper was rolling around all over the floor," Vera explained. "Can you imagine? In church, of all places?"

Iris's first thought was, "What is he up to this time?"

Iris didn't intend to besmirch anyone feeling a sincere desire to grow closer with their Maker, but she had known Raymond Cooper long enough to know when he was up to something.

Vera Penrod was always more than happy to be of assistance, and she was quick to offer a suggestion. "Why not call the story 'Local Celebrity Couple: Cooper and Jesus'?"

Iris had a better idea, though.

Chapter Nineteen

"Silver Tongue"
Fights back

Renderings with Raymond was normally a labor of love for Raymond Cooper. After all, it was his "baby." Reinvented in 1997 as a camouflaged attempt to bolster his clandestine mayoral candidacy, the talk show drew close to half of Lennox Valley's residents each weekday from noon until 3:00. If his show was included in the Neilsen Ratings, Cooper would be almost as popular as *Murder, She Wrote* among Valley folks.

The casual observer would think his plan had worked to perfection. With just under seven weeks until the election, Cooper's most recent antics looked sure to take him to the summit of local politics. Between rising egg prices and inappropriate reading material among Valley youth, Raymond was more popular than ever.

With less than an hour left in his Monday show, Raymond was already looking ahead to some respite during Lennox Valley's second favorite radio program, *Swap Shop*. From time to time callers would interrupt their latest laundry list of items to swap with other listeners to say something about the price of eggs or the "slanted" newspaper editor Iris Long, but on most days *Swap Shop* made for a relaxing change of pace.

It was 2:40 p.m. that fateful Monday, when Raymond took what he thought would be his last call of the day. He generally saved the last ten minutes of the show to deliver a monologue concerning the Federal Reserve System or some other pressing issue.

He answered the call with his usual greeting, "This is Raymond. What's on your mind?"

The caller on the other end stopped Raymond dead in his tracks. He would know that voice anywhere, having heard it hundreds of times.

"Hello, Mr. Cooper," the caller with the familiar, low-toned voice began. "This is Mayor Richard Bland, humble servant of the good folks of Lennox Valley."

There was a discernible pause as Raymond frantically searched through the deepest recesses of his mind for the right words. He barely kept himself from sputtering out, "Well, if it's not 'Silver Tongue' in the flesh!" referring to the nickname of the town mayor, "Silver Tongue" Dick Bland. Luckily, he caught himself before embarrassing himself and the mayor.

Instead, after several awkward seconds, he blurted out, "Well, yes. Hello, Mr. Mayor. Welcome to our show. What's on your alleged 'mind' this afternoon?"

"Well," began 'Silver Tongue,' "This won't take long. I just wanted to congratulate you."

Raymond searched the recesses of his memory. What could the mayor be up to?

"Congratulate me?" murmured Cooper, knowing that Bland's intentions were probably less than sincere.

The mayor's plan was to congratulate Raymond on his newfound faith. After all, Cooper had received no less than six calls on his Monday show in response to his "conversion" at the Lutheran Church the day before.

To his listeners, Raymond's "conversion" at the contemporary service was probably the biggest religious event of the year, ranking ahead of both the arrival of Sarah Hyden-Smith as well as the visit by celebrity TV evangelist Todd Cecil of Revival Flames Ministries.

Mayor Bland began going over his thoughts early that morning. Even with the nickname "Silver Tongue," words didn't always come easily to Bland. Before a speech, he would practice for hours to give the impression that he was a naturally gifted orator. He had practiced much longer than usual for this particular on-air conversation with the town's biggest media celebrity.

The mayor memorized his lines, even writing them down on paper so he wouldn't forget something important. They were a work of art, beginning with, "Isn't it true that you hadn't been to a church service in more than 50 years prior to yesterday? Isn't it true that your motives for joining the church were less than sincere? Isn't it time you were honest with the good folks of Lennox Valley and told them the truth about your so-called 'conversion'?"

Then, with his low, powerful voice, he would force his point, "Isn't it true that the only reason you joined Lennox Valley Lutheran Church was to sway the Christian vote of this community, knowing they would otherwise vote for me?"

Bland may have had a gift for oration, but his abilities didn't compare with Raymond's scheming ways. Cooper was quick. Sure, there was a momentary lapse upon hearing the Mayor's voice, but he recovered quickly. As soon as "Silver Tongue" Dick Bland continued with, "Yes, I just wanted to congratulate you," Cooper immediately shot back with, "Well, thank you, Mayor!"

Without his listeners knowing it, Raymond hung up on Bland and spoke for 14 minutes about the mayor's kind gesture in calling to congratulate him on his "spiritual awakening."

"You have to give it to Mayor Bland," Cooper uttered gleefully into the microphone. "Even with all our differences, he understands that faith goes beyond politics."

"I can't help," he almost whispered as he closed his Monday

show, "but believe that he was divinely inspired to make that call. Thank you, Mayor."

Iris Long and Sarah Hyden-Smith were sharing a few moments over coffee at the Hoffbrau as Raymond's show played over the sound system.

Noticing a sudden change in her friend's complexion, Sarah reached across the booth and placed her hand on Iris's hand.

"Are you okay?" Sarah asked.

"Yes, I'm okay," answered Iris. "There's just something about Raymond Cooper that sets me on edge."

Chapter Twenty

Poet Laureate
Takes aim at Raymond

Small town newspapers are a bit different from their counterparts in New York or Los Angeles. That's true today, and it was true
in 1998, when I was growing up in Lennox Valley.

Unlike papers in the big city, *Lennox Valley Hometown News*
wasn't made up of a large staff of full-time journalists and investigative reporters. The total payroll of our newspaper included Boyd
Sanders, part-time intern, reporter and student at the local junior
college; Maxine Miller, who penned "Rumor Has It," the most
popular weekly column in the paper; and Iris Long, who wasn't
really on the payroll as such.

As editor, publisher and owner of the newspaper, Iris got whatever profit was left after all the bills were paid. Needless to say, she
wasn't rich, but she loved her work and knew that she was involved
in something important. And for what it's worth, that's a lot more
than most folks can say.

Until recently, *Hometown News* had a part-time advertising
person on staff, but demonstrating the power of printed news, she
answered a want ad in her own paper and took a job selling real
estate for an agency based 16 miles away in Springfield.

That left one other staff member, Elizabeth Barrett, "Lennox Valley's Poet Laureate." She would take deference to being called a staff person. It wasn't that she was rude, but she just tended to think of herself in more elevated terms.

It was even rumored that Elizabeth, a widow, had married her late husband, Millard Barrett, just for his last name. In 1997, Maxine took aim at her fellow writer in "Rumor Has It" with the headline, "Could Raleigh Browning be next?"

While Iris covered the hard news, Boyd was sent out to cover city council and school board meetings, high school ball games and church socials. It's hard to express just how boring a school board meeting can be, especially when you're not a board member, and even more so if you have no children in school. At least there were usually refreshments at church socials.

Maxine kept pace with the local rumor mill and was having a banner year in 1998. Her focus had shifted from the "budding romance" between The Valley's two unmarried clergypersons (at least she assumed Sarah Hyden-Smith was single) to the latest murmurings concerning Raymond Cooper's "conversion" at the recent contemporary service at Lennox Valley Lutheran Church. Romance made for good gossip. Religion made for even better gossip.

It was hard, even for a woman of sophistication and savoir-faire, a term Elizabeth liked to use with regularity, to stay above the fray of the recent events of The Valley. It was rare for her to get down into the mud, so you wouldn't find Elizabeth writing about the annual turkey shoot or the TV evangelist coming to town.

Iris asked Elizabeth if she would consider writing a poem when Todd Cecil announced his trip to The Valley. Elizabeth didn't mince words.

"I wouldn't waste my time attempting to find a word that rhymes with 'Cecil'," answered Elizabeth. The whole idea of a poem about a TV evangelist seemed beneath her.

Barrett had a way with words. Her column, titled "Free Verse," always included the subhead, "By our own Poet Laureate, Elizabeth Barrett," underneath.

In 1996, she penned one of her most memorable poems:

There may not be much to see in my small town,
but I tend to not let that bring me down.
For just when it seems no joy is near,
I make up for that with what I hear.

And there was much to hear during that fateful week in Lennox Valley. "Silver Tongue" Dick Bland, town mayor, was furious at Raymond Cooper, who on Monday slyly hung up on Mayor Bland just as he was getting ready to "out" Cooper for joining the Lutheran Church under false pretenses.

All he was able to say, before hearing the click and dial tone, was, "I want to congratulate you."

Now daily listeners of *Renderings with Raymond* were more convinced than ever their champion of the airwaves would soon be their new town mayor. Even the current mayor, Dick Bland, was overcome with the sincerity of Cooper's "conversion." His phone call to congratulate Raymond was proof of that.

But Elizabeth didn't fall for Cooper's performance. She knew something was amiss, and her weekly poem would be the topic of conversation for days to follow:

Talk-show hero Raymond Cooper
fell on the floor in religious stupor.
To some, that makes him mighty super.
Please hand me a pooper scooper.

Brother Jacob livens "No Shoes"

Kevin Slimp's
The Good Folks of Lennox Valley

In 1999, Reverend Billy Joe Raymond was universally recognized as the fieriest preacher in Lennox Valley, with good reason. Not a Sunday, or Wednesday night for that matter, passed at First Baptist Church without an altar call and at least two re-dedications by souls who had wondered astray, ultimately finding their way home during a latter verse of "I Surrender All."

Back in the 60s, Bob Dylan unknowingly prophesied the future of Lennox Valley when he sang, "The Times They Are a'Changin." But change they did, when the Lennox Valley Lutheran Church called Jacob Gehrig, direct descendant Lou Gehrig, to serve as its assistant pastor.

Assistant pastors were a rarity in Lennox Valley. First Baptist Church had an assistant on staff for as long as anyone could remember, but the other churches in town were too small for such gaudy, frivolous, behavior. That all changed with the hiring of "Brother Jacob," as he liked to be called, in 1997.

While associate pastors at First Baptist Church were known to preach a sermon now and then, almost always on Sunday or Wednesday night, Lutherans generally relegated their associates to working with the youth and visiting the sick. That changed in 1998 after Brother Jacob attended a church growth seminar in Kansas City, Missouri, held at a famous Methodist "megachurch."

To hear Brother Jacob tell the story, his heart was strangely warmed at the conference and he felt led to come back to Lennox Valley and begin a "contemporary service" at his church. Contemporary services, usually with drums and electric guitars, were all the rage, as he explained, at Methodist megachurches and he saw no reason they couldn't do

wonders for the ...ley Lutheran C... For sixteen ... had led a grou... who met in th... church at 8:3... to find any d... ists to help w... early risers ... college stud... ends to play...

At least ... about Brot... First, he ... preached, ... even in th... somethin... burning ...

Secon... "paraph... prepar... the hat... he cou... his p... Study... News... fello... brou... ofte... The... len... "L... sc... se...

Raymond Cooper
hatches his "top secret" plan

Kevin Slimp's
The Good Folks of Lennox Valley

Elections have always been big deals in small towns and Lennox Valley is no exception. Winning an elected office is one of the few ways to be a big fish in a community like "The Valley." About your only other options are serving on a church board or getting your picture in the Hometown News.

1998 was an especially contentious election as I remember. You see, it's almost impossible to get re-elected in a small town, unless no one wants to hold your office. It's just too easy to make enemies when you personally know most of your constituency.

A lack of willing candidates is rarely the case, because there's always somebody who wants to be a bigger fish. Raymond Cooper was cast perfectly for the Moby Dick role.

Well, almost perfectly. It was well known that to win an election in Lennox Valley, there was a huge advantage in being a member of First Baptist Church. The Baptist Church was the closest thing to a political machine in our town. With close to 20 percent of the good folks of Lennox Valley on its membership roll and, just as importantly, more than 30 percent of the town's voters, it was hard to win against someone with that many built-in allies.

Raymond, however, had a plan. A few years earlier, he had correctly predicted the upcoming boom in talk radio. He had begun listening to a nationally syndicated radio program based at a station in South Florida and quickly realized the potential of this "new" medium. He took note that listeners were fiercely loyal. No matter the topic, they stood by their host.

At first, Raymond's station was primarily an outlet for sharing his off-the-wall social and political views. But as time passed, he quickly came to see there were additional advantages in owning the town's only radio station.

In 1994, Talk Radio 880 moved to a "round the clock" format, primarily filled with syndicated programming from far away places. The good folks of Lennox Valley were fascinated with stories about UFOs, corrupt politicians and, sometimes, religious programming. It took a lot to fill 24 hours every day.

The most popular show on 880 was "Renderings With Raymond," which could be heard twice each weekday, from noon until 3 p.m. or a repeat of that day's show beginning at 8 p.m. each night.

Most folks considered Raymond a political nutcase, but nutcases tend to attract other nutcases and such was the case with Raymond. It didn't take him long to realize it only required 400 nutcases to win an election in The Valley and that's just what he intended to do.

If he was going to win the mayor's race, beating the incumbent, "Silver Tongue" Dick Bland, and few other yet-to-be-determined opponents, Raymond needed a hot button issue to get voters excited about the next election. He found just the issue.

Beginning in February 1997, "Renderings With Raymond" became a hotbed of fiery conversation centered on the Federal Reserve System. It was sheer genius. Sure, mayors of small towns have no influence on the Federal Reserve System, nor did most people give it much, if any, thought. But Raymond knew he needed only 400 good folks of Lennox Valley to care.

Heated debates concerning the system could be heard daily. Raymond pressed the idea that egg prices had risen 72 percent in just four years, all due to inadequacies in the Federal Reserve System.

Helen Walker was almost in tears as she spoke with Cooper on Tuesday's show. "I won't be able to make my coconut mound cake for the county fair!" she wailed.

In February 1997, no one knew that Raymond Cooper had his eye on the mayor's seat. But as the price of eggs continued to rise, it was only a matter of time until Raymond officially threw his hat into the race.

Chapter Twenty-One

Advice for the New Pastor

Glynn Vickers offers sage advice

It had been three weeks since Reverend Sarah Hyden-Smith made her first appearance in the pulpit of Lennox Valley Methodist Church. In that time, her schedule was filled with unpacking boxes, meeting with committees, preparing her first two sermons and other ministerial duties.

Thanks to the surprise remarks from the Alwood siblings during her first children's sermon, along with the large number of folks who had come out to hear the new preacher, Sarah was feeling pretty good about her first two weeks in The Valley. Still, Sarah knew the newness would eventually wear off, and her attention would turn from getting acquainted with her new surroundings toward shepherding her flock at the Methodist Church.

Three weeks before moving to her new appointment, Sarah made a visit to her predecessor, Glynn Vickers, who had accepted an appointment to another congregation, which he expected to be his last before retiring. She was eager to learn all she could about the Lennox Valley church and gain any insights that could help as she prepared for her position.

Being newer to the ministry, Sarah didn't know much about

Reverend Vickers, but she soon learned he would be an invaluable resource. Glynn was an amiable sort, quick-witted and easygoing. Sarah took a quick liking to him.

Reverend Vickers was a mountain of a man. At 6 feet 8 inches, he towered above just about everyone he met. And at 320 pounds, he was no lightweight. He drove a tan 1994 Chevy Silverado pickup truck. There wasn't a single person in The Valley above three years old who wasn't familiar with that truck. Glynn's wife, Rona, drove a sea green 1996 Buick LeSabre, but it was rare to see Glynn in her car. When they went someplace together, they drove his Silverado.

Their son, Gregg, took after his father. Not quite as tall at 6 feet 7 inches, and not nearly as stout, still there was no doubt whose child he was. He had his dad's sense of humor and love for pickup trucks.

Sarah and Reverend Vickers mostly discussed her new church. Glynn had enjoyed his years there, and Sarah could tell he didn't want to force information on her. It was obvious he respected her as a pastor and didn't want to overstep his boundaries.

Sarah didn't know it until later, but her predecessor made the decision to accept a church 80 miles away in McKinney to serve his remaining years as pastor, rather than finishing out his time in Lennox Valley. As a result of his popularity, he understood it would be hard for anyone else to be accepted as pastor of Lennox Valley Methodist Church while he was still living in the area. He was just that kind of man.

After several minutes, Sarah asked Glynn if he had any advice for her.

He first explained that he was confident Sarah would find her own way and be a very fine pastor for the congregation. After some additional nudging by Sarah, he eventually offered a few pieces of advice.

"I've been in the ministry a long time," Reverend Vickers began. "I know a lot of pastors spend most of their time in meetings and preparing for sermons."

Sarah was on the edge of her seat, hoping for any information that would help her be a better pastor to her new flock.

"It seems to me," he continued, "a few years from now, no one will be able to tell you what happened in a meeting or what was said in a particular sermon. In my four decades in the ministry, I've found that it all comes down to three things. As long as I remembered to do those things, people seemed to like me, and congregations grew."

"He must know what he's talking about," Sarah thought. In her research, she had found that the Lennox Valley church had increased in membership and attendance each year since Glynn arrived. In fact, it had almost doubled in size over the years he served the congregation.

"What are those three things?" asked Sarah.

After pausing briefly, Reverend Vickers said, "First, make a personal visit to the home of every new visitor within two days."

"Two days?" she asked pensively. "Is that even possible?"

"It's important to get to them quickly. That way they know they're important to you. Wait any longer, and they've probably forgotten they even attended. I've found if I can get to them within a couple of days, chances are they will return to church the next Sunday."

"OK. What else?" asked Sarah.

"Visit every member of the church in their homes at least once each year," he said, as if it were common knowledge.

"But how do you find time to prepare for sermons and carry out all your other duties if you're visiting so many people?"

Glynn grinned knowingly, looking down toward the ground. "People will forget your sermon by dinner time. They will remember for years when you visit their home."

Sarah thought hard about what she had just heard. Funny, none of her seminary professors ever talked much about the need to visit the home of visitors so quickly.

"People come to church," he continued, "because they want to matter. And when you go to their homes, they feel like they matter. It's not hard. We have 104 family units in the church. Some live alone, some are families. If you get to two homes each week, you've visited everyone."

Glynn and Rona made a habit of visiting as many first-time attendees as possible together. On Tuesday and Thursday nights, they would get into Glynn's pickup truck and head out to meet with folks in their homes. Sarah began to understand why Reverend Vickers was so popular among the Methodists of The Valley.

Both were quiet for a moment while Sarah digested this new information.

"And what's the third thing?" asked Sarah.

"Visit every member in the hospital every day. And find out if any of your members have a close relative in the hospital, and visit them, too."

"But the nearest hospital is in Springfield," noted Sarah.

Reverend Vickers rubbed his chin and raised his eyebrows, as if to say, "I know. I go there just about every day." However, no words came from his mouth.

Once, Glynn had been invited to the annual conference of the Methodist Church to talk about his advice concerning church growth. It was common knowledge that wherever Glynn and Rona were assigned, the congregation grew.

Sarah left their meeting convinced she would heed his advice. So here she was, three weeks into her first year as pastor, and it was time to start.

While looking over the attendance pads from the most recent Sunday service, Sarah read, "Juliette Stoughton." Next to the name, the box marked "visitor" was checked.

Just below, on the next line, she saw the shaky handwriting belonging to Caroline Hammel, owner of Caroline's Beauty Salon. She had also checked the visitor's box by her name.

It was quite interesting that these two women's names were listed in order on the attendance pad. That meant they were seated side by side in the pew. Since the sanctuary was packed for one of Sarah's first Sundays, they must have been seated close together.

Leaving her office to make her first visits as minister of Lennox Valley Methodist Church, Sarah had no way of knowing that her first visits would be with two strangers who happened to have so much in common.

Before she exited the building, Sarah was met just outside the church office by Beatrice Justice, a peculiar woman wearing a red wool dress and pearls around her neck.

Mrs. Justice had a reputation of being a bit unusual, but not because of how she dressed. Beatrice, Sarah learned, had dropped by the church to pick up a copy of the Upper Room Devotional for a sick friend. At least that's what she told her new pastor.

The real reason for Beatrice's stopover was to get a close-up view of the female preacher. After all, she had never met a female minister up close. Perhaps, she imagined, she might pick up some interesting tidbit concerning Sarah to share with her fellow members of the Lennox Valley Auburn Hat Society.

After a quick introduction, Beatrice asked Reverend Hyden-Smith how she was adjusting to her new home. "Are you liking The Valley so far?"

"I'm finally starting to learn where things are," conceded Sarah. She had no idea how much of an adjustment she was in for.

Her new congregant seemed to focus on Sarah's words, then took her by surprise with her response, which came in the form of a Bible verse: "Exodus 2, verse 22."

At that point, Beatrice nodded, turned and walked out the door.

No pleasantries nor explanation of the verse from Exodus. Reverend Hyden-Smith wasn't sure what to think about the encounter.

Sarah soon realized Beatrice's reputation was well-deserved. Instead of speaking in sentences, like most everyone else, she would often answer with a scripture reference. It could be off-putting at first, but in time Sarah would learn the ways of Beatrice Justice.

It's not so unusual for folks in a place like Lennox Valley to quote scripture now and then. Even Sarah might offer some pastoral advice like, "The Bible says God will not let you be tempted beyond what you can bear," or "Trust the Lord with all your heart."

The difference was Beatrice didn't quote the verses from the Bible. She would just spit out the chapter and verse number, leaving most to wonder what kind of backhanded compliment or advice they had just been given.

Perhaps the most memorable such case was when A.J. Fryerson, who was known to write a weekly letter of complaint to the editor of *Lennox Valley Hometown News*, mentioned Beatrice in one of his tirades.

The next day, Beatrice ran into A.J. just outside the Hoffbrau. In front of at least five witnesses, she looked A.J. straight in the eye and said, "Judges 15, verse 16."

Immediately afterwards, everyone present hurried to find the nearest Bible. A.J. made his way to the Baptist church, less than a block down Main Street.

Heading into the sanctuary, he picked up a pew Bible and found the verse, reading it to himself, "Judges 15, verse 16. 'I have been smitten by the jawbone of an ass!'"

A.J. realized Beatrice Justice was not someone to make light of. He never mentioned her again in a letter to the newspaper editor.

Many folks had noticed it was customary, when Beatrice addressed someone with a Bible verse, a devilish smile would appear on her face, as if she had outwitted her less scripturally educated conversation partner.

Sarah made better than average grades in seminary, and she aced her Old Testament class, but she hadn't quite memorized every word of scripture yet. Walking to her car, Sarah made a mental note to look up Exodus 2:22 later and see what Beatrice was talking about. "Maybe," she thought, "I should brush up on my Old Testament, just to be safe."

Her first stop was the home of Juliette Stoughton. The house looked like many in The Valley. It was white, with an old-fashioned front porch, probably built 30 years before Sarah was born. It was in need of a fresh coat of paint, and a few boards needed replacing, but Sarah wasn't one to judge.

There was a porch swing that hadn't been occupied in some time. A pair of planters with the remains of what used to be azaleas and geraniums nestled against the front edge of the porch coupled with a small table, like the ones you would see in old movies, meant to hold liquid refreshments for those who enjoyed a nice afternoon or evening in the fresh air.

Other than an occasional salesman or someone selling a religion, there hadn't been many visitors to Juliette's home since her soulmate moved on to be with his new soulmate. Juliette recognized her guest immediately from her visit over a week earlier to the Methodist church.

It was apparent to Sarah that Juliette wasn't used to guests dropping by. Juliette seemed a little flustered, but still happy to have company. The pastor had no idea how lonely Juliette was.

It's interesting how two strangers can form an instantaneous bond. She didn't say anything about it, but somehow Juliette knew they were going to be close friends from the moment they met. Once inside, Sarah was surprised to see a Bible on the coffee table.

"That's a beautiful Bible," Sarah said, trying to make small talk.

"I believe it belongs to my landlord," Juliette told her. "I just left it there. I'm sorry it hasn't gotten much use."

"Do you mind if I look at it?" Sarah asked.

At first, Juliette was concerned the new pastor was going to offer a sermon in her living room. As Sarah flipped through the pages intently, Juliette asked, "What are you looking for?"

Sarah faintly replied, "Exodus 2, verse 22."

It was obvious Juliette and Sarah felt comfortable with each other from the beginning. As she thumbed through the Bible on Juliette's coffee table, Sarah shared the bizarre encounter she'd had with Beatrice Justice just before leaving the church.

"What's Exodus 2, verse 22?" asked Juliette after her new friend told her what she was looking for.

"It's a verse in the second book of the Old Testament," answered Sarah. "Exodus is the story of Moses leading his people out of centuries of bondage into a new promised land."

"And that's all she said?" asked Juliette, as puzzled as Sarah. "'Exodus 2, verse 22'?"

"That's it," Sarah almost whispered as she read the scripture silently to herself. "Beatrice asked me how I was getting along in my new hometown. After I told her I was beginning to get used to where things are, she responded with 'Exodus 2, verse 22,' then turned and walked away."

"Well, what's it say?" Juliette was on the edge of her seat.

Sarah read the words aloud slowly, with a bit of a puzzled look on her face, "And he said, 'I have been a stranger in a strange land.'"

"That's pretty strange," Juliette remarked.

"I suppose it is," Sarah responded. "Not particularly bad, just peculiar."

After a moment's pause, Juliette took the lead. "How do you feel about killing animals at church?"

"Do you mean animal sacrifice, like they did in Old Testament days?" asked Sarah.

"No," continued Juliette, "I mean like shooting turkeys every year at the Baptist Church."

Sarah couldn't comprehend what her new friend was talking about. In her few years as a pastor, she had never heard of anyone shooting any kind of animal at church. Eventually, however, she put the puzzle pieces into place.

Juliette was upset about the upcoming men's breakfast and turkey shoot at First Baptist Church. When she first learned about the annual event, Juliette wasn't sure if she was more upset about grown men trampling the church grounds shooting fowl or the idea that women weren't invited. After a couple of months of intense contemplation, she decided she was more upset about the turkeys.

Although Sarah had been assigned to serve the church in Lennox Valley, she hadn't always lived in a small town. Actually, she was more of a big city kind of girl. She explained to Juliette that her mother was one of the early women ministers in the Methodist Church, and now, 30 years later, here was her daughter, pastor of Lennox Valley Methodist Church.

Sarah had moved around a lot, normal for a "PK" (preacher's kid), but had spent most of her teen years in a large city where her mother served as an associate pastor. So, she explained, her understanding of turkey shoots was minimal.

This was 1998, and it wasn't as easy to get information as it is today. Computers weren't plentiful in The Valley, and even if they were, Juliette wouldn't know how to look up such a thing.

Sarah assured Juliette that she would look into details concerning the turkey shoot, still four months away, and let her know what she found. She was, she told her new friend, quite sure that no one would be running around the church grounds looking for turkeys to shoot.

"That just doesn't seem right," Sarah confided, "even for Baptists."

Sarah suggested the two meet for lunch at the Hoffbrau on Friday. It was near the church, and Juliette was familiar with it, even though she hadn't eaten out very often since moving to The

Valley nearly a year earlier.

"I'm off to visit Caroline Hammel," Sarah said as she stood up from the sofa. "Do you know her?"

"No," answered Juliette in a soft tone, "I don't really know much of anyone."

Walking toward Juliette's front door, Sarah paused for a moment, before turning to face her new friend, "Well, now you do."

Smiles made their way across both of their faces.

Chapter Twenty-Two

Hometown News
Uncovers Raymond's dirt

With less than six weeks to go until the "Election of the Century," Raymond Cooper was feeling pretty good about his prospects. His plan, it seemed, was working to near perfection.

First he purchased 880 AM, the town's only radio station, and converted it to an all-talk format. Next, he created his own daily show, highlighting the faults of the current government while enhancing his reputation as defender of the masses. Things seemed to be going exactly as planned for Raymond. In a relatively short period, he had gained a sizable following in The Valley.

By his own count, Raymond needed approximately 430 votes to win the mayoral race in 1998. He estimated somewhere around 600 good folks of The Valley listened to his show, *Renderings with Raymond*, each day. Assuming a majority of those listeners would cast a vote for him, Raymond was feeling pretty good about his chances.

His plan to join the Lutheran Church had been carried out with a precision seldom witnessed in small town politics. The "coup de grâce" was Cooper's handling of Mayor "Silver Tongue" Dick Bland's reaction to his "conversion" during a call to his radio show a week earlier.

Since the beginning, Raymond's biggest concern was Bland's voting bloc at First Baptist Church. Being a member pretty much guaranteed "Silver Tongue" most of the Baptist vote. If Bland could count on the voting Baptists, he would have nearly enough votes to win.

Raymond knew, however, a good number of those Baptists were listening to his daily show. It was critical he sway enough of them into voting for him, primarily by fanning the flames of their fear of the Federal Reserve System. With egg prices consistently creeping up over the past few years, and Raymond placing the blame squarely on the back of the Federal Reserve System, voters were becoming convinced in growing numbers that Cooper was the only viable candidate to stand up to the federal government before it was too late.

Cooper had been especially pleased at Mayor Bland's lack of concern over the Federal Reserve. True enough, it was a completely made-up issue. Raymond spent weeks going over a list of potential controversies to garner allegiance to his show. Other issues that didn't make the cut included concern over government eavesdropping of the World Wide Web, the appropriateness of the early time slot reserved for the wildly popular TV series *Friends* on NBC, and the audacity of the federal government to allow an American space shuttle to dock with a Russian space station.

At one point, he had considered creating a more serious issue out of the Harry Potter book soon making its way to America. Cooper was convinced, however, American children would never be fooled into consuming the writings of a British woman. In addition, when he learned the Potter book was in excess of 200 pages, he knew it couldn't last. No child would read a book that long.

Cooper knew he had found just the thing by combining concern over rising egg prices with mistrust of a federal government that seemed to be losing more control by the minute.

One thing Cooper hadn't counted on, however, was the watchful eye of *Hometown News* editor, Iris Long. She had mistrusted him all along, and his recent "religious conversion" was icing on the cake, as far as she was concerned.

She had written more than one editorial concerning the upcoming election. "How," she wrote in March, "can a small town mayor have any effect on the central banking system of the United States?"

She knew she was preaching to the choir. Most of her loyal readers didn't trust Cooper. However, Raymond's listeners had developed a bias against the media. That is, any media other than Raymond Cooper.

On July 11, during a trip to visit her sister four hours away, Iris realized something was amiss. All along, Raymond had based his rantings on the price of eggs. Over the previous 20 months, the price of a dozen eggs had risen more than 20 cents at the stores in Lennox Valley and Springfield to $1.05. All the fault, Cooper constantly reminded his listeners, of the Federal Reserve System, or "feds," as he liked to say.

During a weekend visit to her sister's home, three hours away, Iris noticed egg prices were 86 cents at the local supermarket. Why, she wondered, would eggs prices be so much higher in Lennox Valley?

As soon as Iris got home, she began working the phone. Remember, this was 1998, and the Internet was in its infancy. Journalists still spent hours on the phone to get a story. That's when Iris realized the truth: Egg prices hadn't risen in places other than Lennox Valley.

How could the Federal Reserve be the culprit if towns and cities outside The Valley weren't affected by rising egg prices? Iris decided to hold the story for another week while she dug further.

In the meantime, Raymond's phone lines were jammed with callers wanting to discuss his "conversion" at the Lutheran Church.

"You are like our knight in shining armor," Cindy Wright

exclaimed. "You never think of yourself, only your town. I don't know what we'd do without you. I knew the Lord was doing great things through you."

"How did it feel?" the show's eighth caller, Marvin Walsh, asked.

"I felt," Cooper answered with a whisper, "like I was totally clean for the first time."

Little did he know Iris Long was about to uncover a little dirt he had missed.

Chapter Twenty-Three

Iris Digs Deeper

Things are about to get egg-citing

Iris Long was perplexed. She had just returned home from visiting her sister four hours away , where she realized that egg prices were 19 cents lower than in her hometown of Lennox Valley. A few phone calls to supermarkets and grocery stores in other cities confirmed her suspicion: Egg prices were more than 20 percent higher in her community than anywhere else she had checked.

Iris had been in the journalism business for a long time. Early in her career, she was actually an investigative journalist for a big-city newspaper. She knew how to dig through the muck to get to the facts.

Sure, she could run a story in this week's paper, blowing the lid wide open concerning egg prices. She could write an editorial, sharing her suspicions that Raymond Cooper was somehow involved. But Iris wanted more than suspicions. She had lived in the same town with Raymond Cooper for decades, and she knew he was an expert at weaseling out of situations just like this. If he had any idea she was on to his scheme, he would somehow explain away his involvement.

She needed more than theories. She needed proof.

At first, she thought Raymond might have somehow convinced the grocery stores in Lennox Valley and Springfield to raise their prices on eggs. But it was unlikely that Cooper could get that many folks to go along with his scheme. Plus, Perry Prince would never go along with such a scheme. There had to be something she was missing.

She searched back through old issues of *The Hometown News* and found the story about Raymond buying the radio station and converting it to an "all talk" format in 1993. She found ads for Perry Prince's store and for the grocery stores in Springfield. Egg prices didn't seem to fluctuate any more than anything else.

That's when it hit her. She searched through the editorial page dating back to June 1996, finding the first letters to the editor concerning the rising price of eggs in the February 12, 1997, issue. Every writer, and there were several of them, mentioned getting their information while listening to *Renderings with Raymond*, Cooper's daily talk show. Raymond had convinced his audience that the Federal Reserve was somehow at fault for high egg prices in Lennox Valley.

Next Iris looked through grocery ads, starting with the June 5, 1996, issue. Egg prices seemed to remain steady through the summer and fall months. Beginning in November, however, there was a two cent increase in the price of a dozen eggs. Moving ahead, she noticed that egg prices rose, almost as if they were scheduled, one cent each month.

"This doesn't seem right," she kept thinking. Why would egg prices suddenly begin rising in Lennox Valley, but nowhere else? Something fishy was going on.

A few pennies might not seem like a lot of money. But a one cent increase each month added up to 21 cents.

Then it dawned on her. All of the stores in Lennox Valley and Springfield bought their eggs from two egg farms located between The Valley and Springfield. One was owned by Marvin Walsh, who Iris recalled, had more than once manned a seat at a display protesting the Federal Reserve System at the Farmers Market.

The other was owned by Elbert Lee Jones, a close friend of Walsh and, Iris remembered, the first to raise a question concerning the Federal Reserve to Pastor Sarah Hyden-Smith during her initial visit to The Valley.

It would be four days until deadline for the next issue of *Hometown News*. Iris suspected they would be busy days, and she was quite sure she would be making visits to see both Elbert Lee and Marvin to discuss the rising price of eggs.

Raymond Cooper was feeling pretty good about himself as he took to the airwaves Friday at noon. After all, with just a little over four weeks until the mayoral election, Cooper felt like he could almost hear the victory celebration that would take place at the VFW Post on Highway 11, just south of town.

Little did he know as he began his opening monologue, Iris Long was leaving the office of *Hometown News* to make the drive to visit Marvin Walsh, one of two farmers who controlled nearly all egg production in The Valley. Marvin lived just two miles west of town toward Springfield, the county seat.

Cooper began his monologue with a brief prayer, a habit that began with his recent "conversion" at the Lutheran Church. Unbeknownst to his listeners, all of his prayers were read from *Eerdmans' Book of Famous Prayers,* a favorite of pastors that contained prayers taken directly from scripture and from famous Christian figures through the centuries.

Today's prayer came from Augustine of Hippo, although listeners assumed it was from the humble soul of Raymond himself:

O Lord, the house of my soul is narrow; enlarge it,
that you may enter in.
It is ruinous, O repair it!
Cleanse me from my secret faults, O Lord,
and spare Your servant from strange sins.

Raymond thought it was one of his best. So good, he imagined, that more than a few Baptists in his listening audience changed their votes as he prayed. Augustine of Hippo, who died in 430 AD, was probably turning in his grave.

Just as Cooper began his daily "Egg Report," where egg prices in Lennox Valley were explored at length, Iris pulled into Marvin Walsh's gravel driveway.

It was part of her job to know everyone in The Valley, and Iris recognized both pickup trucks parked side by side. The red Silverado with the extended cab belonged to Walsh. The black Dodge Dakota, also with an extended cab, belonged to none other than Elbert Lee Jones, the other Valley egg farmer.

Iris felt like she had hit the jackpot. She had imagined she would have to work on Walsh, then make a trip to visit Jones, who lived south of town on Highway 11. Hopefully, she would be able to dig the truth about egg prices out of one of them. As an experienced investigative reporter, though, she knew it would be easier to trap both of them while they were together. She grinned knowingly as she put her car into park.

Marvin and Elbert Lee were sitting in rockers on Walsh's front porch as Iris approached.

Marvin stood and offered a friendly, "Good afternoon, Ms. Long," as she approached the porch. "Selling papers door to door these days?"

Elbert Lee was the quiet one in the group.

"No, I'm not selling papers," she answered with a smile, "but I am working on a story that is bound to sell a lot of papers. Not just here in Lennox Valley, but all over the county."

"That must be some story," said Walsh, a bit less enthused. He suddenly had a bit of concern in his expression. "What is it about?"

"I'm working on a story about two farmers in our community who have conspired to inflate the price of eggs for the past two years."

"Now, hold on," Marvin shot back. "What in the world would make you write a story like that?"

"I thought it only fair to give you the opportunity to shed some light on the subject. It's becoming fairly obvious that you two have concocted quite a scheme. Your neighbors are going to talk about this for years."

Elbert Lee was suddenly interested as he rose from his chair, "Now, hold on just a cotton-pickin' minute . . . "

"Careful, Elbert Lee," said Walsh as he put his hands on his friend's shoulders.

"Careful, nothin'," Elbert Lee barked. "Don't blame this on us. It wasn't our idea."

"Then whose idea was it?" asked Long.

"That doggone radio man. That's who."

With that, Iris Long felt the need to take a seat while she caught her breath. She knew immediately this scoop would make the Sarah Hyden-Smith story pale in comparison.

In all the years Iris Long had served as editor of *Hometown News*, she had never felt faint while covering a story. Never, that is, until she stood on Marvin Walsh's porch and listened as Elbert Lee Jones placed the blame for inflated egg prices directly on the shoulders of Raymond Cooper, local celebrity and aspiring politician.

As she sat to catch her breath, she realized the significance of what had just taken place. This story could destroy Cooper's credibility within the community. At least half of The Valley listened to *Renderings with Raymond* each weekday and saw the host as their knight in shining armor. Their champion was about to lose his most valuable weapon, and the ensuing reaction was impossible to predict.

Being Friday, it was four long days before the next issue of *Hometown News* would go to press. How in heaven's name could she keep the story from leaking before Tuesday? She knew four days would be plenty of time for Cooper to weasel out of this predicament, just as he had many others.

As she sat in her car in Walsh's driveway before driving away, she considered her options. To Iris, the most likely scenario was the two farmers rushing over to Cooper's radio station to tell him what had just happened. Elbert Lee was furious, and she didn't imagine he would be able to contain his rage at being implicated in the scheme. They might keep quiet, she thought, hoping Raymond would take the fall, but that wasn't likely. The good folks of Lennox Valley weren't known for keeping quiet.

As she started her car, she heard Raymond beginning hour two of his Friday show. It was unusual for Raymond to have a guest, as it took away from time for him to lecture his audience about the plight of local government, rising egg prices, illicit involvement by federal agencies and the "radical" press that was more interested in selling newspapers than informing the public. But on this Friday, he was joined by Brother Jacob, associate pastor of Lennox Valley Lutheran Church.

Brother Jacob expected to discuss upcoming activities at the church and answer spiritual questions from callers. He had been studying his Bible even more fervently, anticipating some of the scriptural questions that might come up on the show.

Raymond had something else in mind.

"Pastor," began Cooper, "it is a pleasure to have you in my humble studio. You have made quite the impression on our community in your short time with us."

After exchanging a few pleasantries, Cooper moved straight to his first question: "Did you happen to hear my prayer to begin the show today?"

Brother Jacob responded he had heard the prayer and, for some odd reason, it seemed familiar.

"No doubt," Raymond shot back. "We are both called to serve

104

by the same Lord, and we undoubtedly hear similar phrases echo from his voice as he inspires us. I wouldn't be surprised if we prayed similar prayers every morning."

Cooper didn't want his pastor to remember that the prayer was uttered by a famous church leader about 1600 years earlier, so he quickly moved on to another subject. "Let me ask you something. Do you buy a lot of eggs, Pastor?"

By then, Iris had begun her drive back to town. As she heard Raymond's words, she almost stopped the car to take it all in. She could barely believe what she was hearing, but having known Cooper for more years than she cared to remember, she knew she wasn't dreaming.

Hometown News had printed only two special editions in all the years Iris had been editor, and one was just over two months earlier when news broke concerning the appointment of Sarah Hyden-Smith. Iris hated to give Cooper days to spin his version of the story before hers came out in print. On the other hand, she knew she needed more facts before printing the story. As it was, it would be Elbert Lee's word against Raymond's, and Iris knew Jones didn't stand much of a chance in a fair battle.

"I bought four dozen eggs for the children's Easter egg hunt at the church," Brother Jacob acknowledged. "The children got a lot of joy while dyeing the eggs. Otherwise I don't normally purchase many eggs. Maybe a dozen every few weeks."

"You know," countered Raymond, "our country was founded on the separation between church and state. But it sounds to me like the actions of the state are causing our church to spend too much for Easter eggs."

"I guess I wouldn't know much about that," muttered the pastor.

"I suppose," Raymond quickly responded, "that's why the good Lord sent me to you."

A slight grin came across Cooper's face as he continued the

conversation.

"You know, Pastor," Raymond went on, "We make a pretty good team for the Lord."

Iris felt a bit dazed as she listened to the conversation between Cooper and Jacob.

"Heavens," Iris whispered to herself. "Heavens."

Chapter Twenty-four

Breaking News!
Egg case cracked wide open

I've always said that gossip in Lennox Valley was born in one of three places: Maxine's weekly column, "Rumor Has It," Raymond Cooper's radio show, or Caroline's Beauty Salon.

Being a Friday afternoon, every seat in Caroline's was filled, and all the hair dryers were humming as the good ladies of The Valley prepared to look their best for Sunday services. Some would call it coincidence that the women were trying to discuss Maxine's latest installment of "Rumor Has It" as *Renderings with Raymond* was playing in the background on the ancient sound system. All three ingredients were in the mix for a gossip-fest of gigantic proportions.

There's a tradition among gossip columnists called the "blind item." When a columnist gets a juicy tip but doesn't have a reliable source, as was often the case in "Rumor Has It," a blind item is sometimes applied. Maxine used this technique frequently, describing in detail something that had happened to someone in The Valley without revealing any names.

For example: "What single minister in Lennox Valley was seen having lunch with another 'supposedly' single pastor at the Hoffbrau last Monday?"

The salon was full of customers trying to discuss Maxine's column while listening to Raymond as he concluded his second hour of programming with Brother Jacob as his guest.

"I believe we are," exclaimed Raymond, "cut from the same cloth, Brother Jacob." Then, after a dramatic pause, "Wouldn't you agree?"

Jacob attempted to sputter some words, but Raymond cut him off before he had a chance. "We should do this again," continued Raymond. "It's a nice change to have someone with me to discuss important theology."

Not that anyone noticed besides Jacob, but his contribution to the discussion amounted to a total of three minutes and twelve seconds during the second hour of Raymond's show. He secretly hoped he'd never be subjected to such torture again.

Vera Penrod, who was under the hair dryer closest to the window overlooking Main Street, interrupted the discussion about "Rumor Has It" as she noticed something peculiar happening across the street. She saw two figures approaching the radio station just down the street.

"Look at that Elbert Lee Jones and Marvin Walsh scurrying into the radio station like a couple of mice," she said in a distasteful tone. "They almost knocked over that young Lutheran pastor. I wonder what they're up to now."

A hushed tone suddenly covered Caroline's as everyone waited to hear what Raymond would have to say after the "top of the hour" commercial break. Vera broke the silence as she said, "I wonder if Elbert Lee and Marvin have some breaking news."

Top of the hour commercial breaks generally lasted four minutes on Cooper's show. The salon assembly couldn't help but notice when the commercial for Massengale's Mortuary played a second time. They had heard the familiar phrase hundreds of times through the years: "When the friendly faces from Massengale's Mortuary knock on your door, let them in. There's always time to discuss plans for your own funeral."

Eventually, after seven minutes, Raymond returned to the air. "You know," he uttered, "that visit with Brother Jacob has me feeling extra spiritual this afternoon. I think this would be a good time to play a few gospel songs for our listening audience so you can share in my sacred moment." Vera suspected he was just buying time.

The salon was buzzing with anticipation. The customers at Caroline's listened intently as Raymond finally returned to the air, following "O For a Thousand Tongues to Sing."

"Friends," began Raymond, "I have the biggest news flash in Lennox Valley history. I'll be right back with the details after 'Trust and Obey' and 'Rock of Ages,' two personal favorites."

The ladies in Caroline's Beauty Salon were on pins and needles. They knew it must be related to the sight of Elbert Lee Jones and Marvin Walsh scurrying into the radio station just minutes earlier.

While all the good ladies in Caroline's were getting their hair just right for Sunday services, Iris Long, editor of *Lennox Valley Hometown News*, was sitting down at her desk to write what might be the most important story of her career.

With four days before *Hometown News* went to press, Iris knew it would have taken a miracle for Marvin and Elbert Lee to keep the news from Cooper that Jones had just confessed to being part of an egg price-fixing scheme hatched by none other than Raymond Cooper himself.

That's when Long heard Raymond's announcement about the upcoming news flash. Her heart sank. She had dealt with The Valley's most prominent celebrity long before he bought the town's only radio station and ran for mayor. Cooper was notorious for getting himself into trouble and, just as quickly, finding a way to escape the consequences of his actions.

Iris took her fingers off the keyboard and waited. There was nothing more for her to do.

Back at the radio station, the frantic atmosphere had calmed a bit. In the background, the old gospel hymn "Trust and Obey" played. Raymond had told his listening audience a few minutes earlier that he had been inspired by his conversation with the previous on-air guest, Brother Jacob, to play a few gospel tunes. In reality, he needed time to scheme.

A few moments earlier, as Jacob exited the station's front door, Marvin and Elbert Lee almost knocked the young pastor over as they hurried into the lobby while "top of the hour" commercials were playing over the air. Inside the radio studio, emotions turned frantic as Marvin explained how Elbert Lee had spilled the beans to Iris.

"What has gotten into you?" blared Raymond as his winded friends caught their breath.

"Elbert Lee has gone and done it this time," Marvin shot back.

"Gone and done what, Marvin?" Cooper asked, confused at what was happening.

"He told that newspaper lady that you were behind the egg price deal."

"Wait. He did what? Hold on. Exactly what did he say?" asked Cooper.

Marvin answered, "He said it was 'that radio man's fault.'"

"That was all he said?" asked Cooper.

"Wasn't that enough?" Walsh shot back. "She asked about us fixing the egg prices, and Elbert said it was 'that radio man's idea' all along."

Cooper told his fellow schemers to calm down. "Give me a minute to think," he said coolly.

And think he did. Raymond always had an idea. The more trouble he seemed to get out of, the more his listening audience praised him as their champion. Cooper knew he just needed the right angle.

As the final hymn played, Raymond heard the words of the gospel favorite playing on air, "Be of sin the double cure. Save from wrath and make me pure."

As the final chorus of the hymn played, Raymond went over the plan one last time with the two farmers. Elbert Lee was having such a hard time staying calm that Cooper finally told him to go sit in the lobby.

Word had spread throughout the town, and more than two-thirds of the good folks of Lennox Valley were sitting by their radios waiting for the news flash. Most guessed someone had died. Others thought the Federal Reserve might be overthrowing the town government.

"Welcome back, friends," Raymond began. "I now know why the good Lord led me to play those calming tunes a moment ago. He must have known what was about to happen."

Iris could hardly believe her ears. Just how was Cooper going to get out of this mess?

Cooper continued, "I'm sitting in the studio with Marvin Walsh and Elbert Lee Jones, two respected farmers and leaders of our community. They've come to me, wanting to confess something to all the good folks in our Valley."

You could have heard a pin drop in Caroline's Beauty Salon as everyone listened.

"It seems," continued Raymond, "that my prayer earlier in the show caused these two to do some real soul-searching. Elbert Lee just told me they felt led to come here to tell the citizens of our community that, while the egg price increases were primarily due to issues with the Federal Reserve, they do feel some personal responsibility for the rise in egg prices over the past two years in

111

our community."

Iris sank in her seat.

Chapter Twenty-Five

Turn Your Radio On
Listen to the music in the air

In 1937, Albert E. Brumley wrote a catchy gospel tune titled "Turn Your Radio On," which was eventually recorded by dozens of artists and groups, including Skeeter Davis in the 1960s and Ray Stevens a decade later.

Like many hit songs, "Turn Your Radio On" reappeared from time to time, possibly because radio stations loved playing the self-celebrating tune so much. Most folks under 50 won't remember, but there was a time when all but a few radio stations didn't begin each day until sunrise, and many of those stations in small towns across America began their days with that favorite gospel melody.

While it was recorded numerous times by well-known artists, no one had a bigger hit with the song than Tangi Blevins & the Heavenly Hosts. Tangi was a sweet, 30ish, dark-haired woman with a smile that lit up the room when the song first hit the air, and her fans still loved her voice and her precious smile.

"Turn Your Radio On" touched many hearts in The Valley and across America. When Tangi sang the chorus, you knew she meant every word. The song was all about sharing Heaven's glory and getting in touch with God, simply by turning the radio on.

While a lot of folks in The Valley were fixated on the upcoming mayoral election, there were others who had their thoughts focused on another major August event: The Spring County Fair. The fair was the biggest annual event in Spring County and gave us the opportunity to have a last bit of fun before school began for the fall session.

For teenagers like Mary Ann Tinkersley and me, the fair meant getting our plants and animals prepared. There was a lot of pride involved in winning a ribbon, and we took the opportunity seriously.

Mary Ann and I were getting our lambs ready for the annual FFA judging, a big milestone for small-town youth. We met near the town square each evening throughout the summer to walk Archibald and Snowflake, and it was paying off in more ways than one.

I was getting to spend time with the prettiest girl in all of Lennox Valley, and the lambs were looking more contest-worthy every day.

Most of the excitement about the upcoming fair, especially among the female population, was reserved for the lineup of pseudo-celebrities who made their way through the county fair circuit each year. Other than that, the closest The Valley would come to seeing real celebrities would be when a former country or gospel star would make their way to Springfield, the county seat, and perform at the civic auditorium. The civic auditorium, like a lot of venues in that period, was built by the Civilian Conservation Corps, a public work relief program that operated during the Great Depression.

One great thing about fair entertainment was the cost. It was free with a paid admission to the fair. Admission was only three dollars if you entered before 4:00, so it was possible to see more than one star in the same week.

Some fair headliners were bigger than others. No one will ever forget Tim Jones, the Tom Jones impersonator, who caused more than one fainting spell as he sang "She's a Lady" in 1977.

If I tried to name the biggest star to grace the stage at the Spring County Fairground before 1998, it most likely would have been a toss-up between 1985's Boxcar Willie, who catapulted to fame as an overalls-wearing hobo selling records during afternoon Brady Bunch reruns, and "Mr. Sound Effects" Wes Harrison in 1983.

But on Tuesday, July 21, 1998, the primary focus of attention shifted from weekend news of the spiritual re-dedication of Elbert Lee Jones and Marvin Walsh during the Sunday contemporary service at the Lutheran Church, to the posters being hung in store windows along the town square.

Who could believe it? In just four weeks, Tangi Blevins, along with both Heavenly Hosts, would be appearing live on stage at the county fair. This could just be the biggest thing to happen at the county fair since Boxcar Willie. This surely made the 11-mile journey to the county fairgrounds worth the effort.

Raymond Cooper, thankful for anything that would temporarily divert the community's attention away from the recent egg-price scandal, found an old 45 rpm in the record vault left from the previous station owner. Earl Goodman, delivering mail to homes on 3rd street, noticed the tune playing as he walked past each screen door on this warm summer day. It was Tangi Blevins, singing "Turn Your Radio On."

He thought it was odd, since Raymond Cooper generally gave his daily Federal Reserve Report at 2:45. Whatever the reason, Earl couldn't get the song out of his head the rest of the day.

And to think, all this happened as Iris Long made the final touches to the next morning's edition of *The Lennox Valley Hometown News*. Pasting the headline was the final piece of work necessary to finish the paper.

Just like most big events in the summer of '98, chatter about

Tangi Blevins would wind down in favor of something much bigger.

Iris Long inhaled, then exhaled, as she made the final touches to the front page. This was certainly turning out to be a big year for news in The Valley.

Chapter Twenty-Six

Juliette

Soulmate memories haunt Juliette

Loneliness lasts. It never completely goes away. It is the one emotion that seems to make its way into the hearts of almost every man and woman at some point during a lifetime. Sure, it can be masked. Other people and interests partially fill the void, but now and then loneliness seems to find its way back when least expected.

Juliette Stoughton knew all about loneliness, and for some reason, it had just dawned on her an anniversary was approaching. It was an anniversary she would just as soon forget.

August 4, 1998, would mark one year to the day since Juliette moved to Lennox Valley to be with her soulmate, Chris Roadhouse. And as soulmates often do, Chris soon left her to be with his new soulmate, a younger woman he met while attending a national leadership conference for book dealers in Des Moines, Iowa.

Juliette was no stranger to loneliness. Married at 21, she found herself 32 and single with no children 11 years later. In the 12 years since the divorce in 1986, Juliette had tried dating a few times. This was before computer dating became the rage. There were no online dating sites to speak of, and it was a little harder to find potential suitors.

At one point, she thought she had found "the one." That all changed when she learned "the one" she was so sure about had secretly planned a romantic cruise for two to Hawaii, and she wasn't invited. To make matters worse, she found about the trip on her own, four days before the happy couple set sail on Hawaiian Cruise Line's ship appropriately named "Independence."

Juliette thought she would never get over the experience, but time is a funny thing. As William Shakespeare once wrote, "Better three hours too soon than a minute too late."

She did her best to put Russell Mickelson behind her. He was a lowlife, a scoundrel, someone best forgotten. She tried to remind herself a man like Russell could never be trusted. Even if she had married him, he was the kind of person who would always keep his options open, whether she was aware of it or not.

Eventually, she marked what she later called "the Hawaii event" to experience, thankful that she found out before it was too late and she was married to a man who might secretly take other women on ocean voyages.

A year later she met Chris Roadhouse. Blond and blue-eyed with a big smile, he looked the part of a future soulmate. They met, interestingly enough, at a personal growth conference in Nashville, Tennessee. Juliette was there to hear her favorite self-help guru speak on "Attracting the Positive and Deflecting the Negative." Chris was working at a vendor's booth, selling copies of the speaker's latest book to excited buyers.

Fresh from a session titled "Finding Your Soulmate," Juliette stood five deep in line, waiting for her turn to buy a copy of *Colossal Steps*. She felt sure she would return two hours later when, for ten dollars, she would meet the author as he signed her just-purchased copy.

Little did she know that less than a year later, she would be packing almost everything she owned and moving to a small town three states away to be with her real soulmate. After all those years of searching, she had found "the one," and Chris was worth the wait. Well, so she thought.

Juliette sat in her living room, shades partially pulled so the room was a bit dark, listening to her favorite song from her teen years, "Operator" by Jim Croce.

As she listened to Jim sing to the operator about the love he had lost, she understood what he was talking about. Like the singer, it made her cry every time she thought about Chris Roadhouse and the love he'd left behind.

As Juliette thought about the past, Iris Long was busy finalizing the pages for the next day's edition of *Hometown News*. Iris had written and rewritten the headline to accompany what was sure to be a big story. After rewriting the headline more than a dozen times, Iris finally settled on:

Cooper Lays an Egg Following Price Fiasco

On the Opinion page, Iris penned an 800-word editorial titled "Is There Anyone Out There?" In paragraph three, she wrote, "Surely there is someone worthy of leading our Valley into the future without lies, tricks and deceit."

Iris was no stranger to politics. She was a seasoned journalist, one who knew the ropes. The Valley was at a crucial point in time, a time when serious leadership was needed. This was the type of column for which Iris was best known.

She added that Dick Bland was a "fine man," but would have a hard time defeating Cooper. Cooper was slippery and knew how to cover his tracks, so his unpopular deeds went unnoticed.

She reminded the voters it wasn't too late. The statute for mayoral elections allowed candidates to place their names on the ballot as late as 21 days before the election. That meant there was just one week before the deadline.

"The qualifications are as follows: At least 28 years of age, no felony convictions, and a resident of Lennox Valley for 12 months."

"If you are reading this," Iris concluded, "step up now. Not just for yourself, but for all of Lennox Valley."

Chapter Twenty-Seven

Iris Plots Her Strategy

Can Raymond get away with this?

These might have been the most memorable six days of my teenage years. Between Friday, July 17, and Tuesday, July 21, 1998, Iris Long had broken the egg price-fixing story wide open; Raymond Cooper had quickly devised a sinister scam to convince his listeners he wasn't involved in the price scandal; the good folks of The Valley learned one of the biggest gospel groups of all time would be playing at the county fair in just four weeks; and both Elbert Lee Jones and Marvin Walsh had publicly rededicated their lives to the Lord during the contemporary service at the Lutheran Church.

In case you are keeping count, that's five days. Then there was Wednesday.

Iris Long knew Raymond Cooper's cover story was a sham. It has been said "all is fair in love and war," and Raymond had no time for love while he was still deep in the trenches of an election battle. Like any good journalist, Iris believed in the public's right to know. She would include the facts on the front page, with her own thoughts on the Opinion page.

Iris knew most sentiments would remain unchanged. It would

take more than a few words from the "biased media" for Cooper devotees to turn on their champion. Most "Raymondites," as they had come to be called, couldn't understand why the media, which included only *The Hometown News* in Lennox Valley, was so prejudiced against their faithful, humble servant.

As hard as it is to imagine, there were other things going on in the lives of the good folks of Lennox Valley. There were some who hadn't even read the morning paper and had no idea who would be performing at the county fair. There were even a few that hadn't been following Cooper's renderings each day from noon until 3:00. Yes, some folks in Lennox Valley had lives. Lives that extended beyond entertainment and politics.

As Juliette sat across the booth from Sarah Hyden-Smith, sipping hot tea and memorizing the Hoffbrau's dessert menu, neither she nor Sarah had any suspicion this conversation would alter their friendship in so many ways. After all, they had only known each other a short time.

From outward appearances, they didn't have a lot in common. Sarah was a minister, with a degree from a famous Methodist seminary in Ohio as proof.

Eventually, Juliette lowered her guard enough to share something she had been hiding from her new friend. "I need to tell you something. Something really important."

"Okay," responded Sarah in a caring tone.

She explained to Sarah that her old life was much different. Before moving to The Valley, she had a good job. She was involved in several community causes. She told how she'd fallen in love with her soulmate and moved to The Valley.

Jessie Orr had been a waitress at the Hoffbrau for as long as anyone could remember. She had that special talent for hearing everything without hearing anything. Along with this talent, she had the knack for knowing when to butt in and when to keep her distance.

This was the perfect time to butt in, Jessie thought. "It says in today's paper there's still time for someone to get their name on the ballot for the mayor's race."

Neither Juliette nor Sarah understood the connection to their discussion.

"You've been here a year. You're obviously over 28 years old. Maybe you should consider running," Jessie explained to her befuddled patrons.

Conversation stopped as Jessie took her time refilling the cups. Sarah and her new friend paused to digest the possibility of a "Juliette Stoughton for Mayor" campaign.

"You know," said Sarah, "that might not be as crazy as it sounds. There certainly needs to an option besides our current mayor and Raymond Cooper."

"You've got the pastor behind you!" quipped Jessie. "You could make badges that say 'I'm votin' for Stoughton!'"

Finally, everyone relaxed and chuckled at the thought. Maybe Jessie would be The Valley's next poet laureate.

Across the town square, as Raymond, Elbert Lee and Marvin huddled together at the radio station, they read Iris Long's editorial, having no idea looming just over the horizon might be a bigger problem than a few cracked eggs.

Sarah apologized for leaving, but she had to go to her first meeting with The Valley clergy. She didn't want to make a bad impression by arriving late.

Every fifth Friday of the month, which generally comes around about four times most years, the clergy of The Valley would gather together for lunch. An informal affair, the group eventually adopted a name. Somewhere in the early 1990s, the gathering came to be known as the Ministerial Alliance of Lennox Valley.

To outsiders, meaning just about anyone who doesn't work for one of The Valley churches, the words "Ministerial Alliance" bring thoughts of important discussions concerning major theological and ethical issues. The pastors are careful to be sure the meeting is included in each of their respective church newsletters, and the good folks of the Baptist, Catholic, Lutheran and Methodist churches can feel relief that their shepherds are guarding against any corrupt influences that might infiltrate their community.

To the clergy of The Valley, however, the Ministerial Alliance basically means a chance to have lunch together and compare notes about what's going on in their congregations.

The members of the group realized early on there was danger in announcing the meeting so prominently among their flocks. Now and then, members of the community requested an opportunity to address the Alliance, usually to bring to their attention some moral concern requiring their collective wisdom and guidance.

It didn't take long for the pastors to realize the necessity of planning a "business meeting" after lunch to allow members of the community to address the group. Otherwise, the respected leaders would never be able to discuss politics, sports or other matters of great importance.

So it was on July 31, 1998, the ecclesiastical leaders of the community gathered together for lunch. This would be the first Alliance meeting for Sarah Hyden-Smith, and she approached the date with a combination of excitement and trepidation. After all, she was the first female to enter the all-male fraternity of ministers in Lennox Valley, and she was concerned she might not be welcomed with open arms.

Iris Long, quickly becoming Sarah's confidante, told her to "stop stressing, and enjoy lunch with your colleagues."

Sarah decided to take her advice. Making her way into Betsy's Diner, she was pleasantly surprised by her reception. All her colleagues, even those from churches that didn't allow female clergy, offered their sincere welcome and quickly made her feel at home.

Father O'Reilly was the first to welcome Sarah as she entered Betsy's on Highway 11, just north of the VFW. The group usually lunched at Betsy's instead of the Hoffbrau to keep the Baptists and some Methodists from getting upset at their pastors for eating at an establishment that served beer. As Sarah was beginning to learn, most of her congregation wasn't concerned about her having a beer at lunch, but she was aware there were a few who would mind.

Sarah briefly considered raising the subject of the annual Men's Breakfast and Turkey Shoot at First Baptist Church, but she soon thought better of the idea. After all, what concern of hers was it if men wanted to have a meal together and shoot things? Maybe after a year, the time would be right to address such things before the group, but she seemed to be getting along with her fellow clergy and desperately wanted to fit in.

Most of the meal was spent discussing the upcoming election, with Father O'Reilly taking a good bit of ribbing for having the only church without a candidate on the ballot.

"Looking at the candidates," quipped "the good father, "I'm thinking I should round one up."

Following lunch, the group began their business meeting in the "social room" at Betsy's. The social room was a fancy name for four tables that could be separated from the rest of the diner with an accordion-style folding wall.

There was one item of business on the meeting schedule, a presentation from Vera Penrod, representing the Auburn Hat Society. Mrs. Penrod was a regular at these meetings, and each clergyperson stood to greet her as she entered the room. It was her second meeting with Sarah, having attended the gathering at the Methodist Church a week before Sarah's first Sunday in The Valley.

"You might remember," Penrod began, "earlier this year I brought an item to your attention about a scandalous book that will soon be read by many of our children."

Being new to the alliance, Sarah had no idea what book Vera

was referring to.

"Harry Potter," continued Penrod, "might be the most dangerous element to prey upon our youth since Dungeons and Dragons was banned from official school activities in 1978."

Being a fan of Harry Potter, Sarah almost giggled before catching herself.

Vera continued, "I have spoken to both Raymond Cooper and Mayor Bland, and both agree that something must be done about this menace. I'm sure you will give this issue the prayerful consideration it warrants."

Lutheran Pastor Brother Jacob, sitting next to Sarah, leaned over and whispered, "Welcome to Lennox Valley."

Chapter Twenty-Eight

Pre-Election Events
A battle is brewing

With seven days remaining until the mayoral "Race of the Century," groups gathered throughout Lennox Valley to cheer on their candidates.

Knowing where your bread is buttered is an important skill in the political arena. "Silver Tongue" Dick Bland held his campaign gala in the First Baptist Church fellowship hall, where 200 supporters gathered to celebrate his upcoming victory. Red, white and blue streamers hung throughout the room, alongside photos of Bland glued to letter-size sheets of red, white and blue construction paper. All who gathered knew "Silver Tongue" had at least two advantages in the race.

First, he hadn't angered many good folks over the past four years, which was quite the accomplishment for an incumbent in The Valley. If it hadn't been for the furor over egg prices and the Federal Reserve System, folks would have been hard-pressed to name any issue at all that had divided the community over the previous four years.

It hadn't hurt that Bland rarely took a side in divisive issues. Though his speeches were eloquent, they were mostly meant to inspire the town, not to address any important matter.

Bland's second advantage was self-evident. He had been a member of First Baptist Church as long as anyone could remember. Everyone in the room other than Iris Long, who was covering the event for *Hometown News*, was quite certain God was on Dick's side. After all, he was a loyal churchgoer, having 17 years of Sunday school "perfect attendance" pins to show for it. Those pins don't come easily. Often were the Sundays he would show up with a cold or other ailment in an effort to keep his streak alive. With God on his side, the mayor was a shoo-in.

The gala began with a somber yet powerful prayer by the church's pastor, Brother Billy Joe Prather. That was followed by a rousing rendition of "Onward Christian Soldiers," sung by the attendees and accompanied by Loraine Sutherland, First Baptist Church pianist. Unlike the Methodists, who were lucky to find trained musicians in their congregation, pianists were plentiful among the parishioners at First Baptist Church.

Two miles away, on Highway 11, there was another celebration taking place. The VFW was the perfect spot for Raymond Cooper's "Campaign Bash," as he had referred to it during his radio talk show the past few days. Other than an opening salvo by the VFW chaplain, there were no prayers at Raymond's celebration. There were no choirs or hymns. There were, however, tipsy veterans mixing alongside Raymond's most fervent supporters. And, instead of hymns, the two cracked speakers in the jukebox blared "All My Exes Live in Texas." There was singing, however, as a few of the celebrants crooned along with George Strait.

Earlier that afternoon, Juliette Stoughton held a less animated event than her opponents. Supported by her friend and pastor, Sarah Hyden-Smith, along with Iris Long, the only Valley voter who would attend two election celebrations that day, Juliette listened as the two of them discussed campaign strategy. She listened intently, all the while knowing her chances of winning were someplace between slim and none. Let's face it, Juliette was a newcomer to

Lennox Valley and didn't have an entire church or a radio audience aiming to get her elected.

Fortunately, Iris and Sarah were able to convince Juliette the annual First Baptist Church Men's Breakfast and Turkey Shoot should not be an issue in the campaign. Long explained she planned to endorse a candidate in the upcoming edition of *The Hometown News* as she did in every mayoral election. Juliette would simply have to come up with something more newsworthy than pancakes and turkeys as a suitable campaign platform.

Iris was a credible journalist. She wouldn't simply hand her official support over to Juliette. The upstart candidate would have to earn it.

Other than a story announcing Juliette's campaign in the previous edition of the paper, there had been little notice of her candidacy. Cooper, obviously aware her chances of winning were minuscule at best, ignored Juliette's campaign after initially reacting to the news when she entered the race. "Silver Tongue" seemed content to focus on his main adversary, Raymond Cooper.

Her opponents were crafty campaigners. With Cooper running on the slogan, "In your heart, you know he's right," borrowed from Barry Goldwater's 1964 presidential campaign, and Bland sticking with the rallying cry from his first race, "Stand with Bland," Juliette needed a catchy and memorable slogan, something to help voters recognize she was a viable candidate.

Jessie, waitress at the Hoffbrau, was one of a handful of curious villagers who made their way to Juliette's event.

"How about this?" Jessie chimed in. "Vote for the most egg-cellent candidate, Juliette Stoughton!"

"Now, that's funny," quipped Sarah.

"You know, that just might work," Iris chimed in. "It's funny, and it reminds voters of Raymond's involvement in the egg scandal."

Four hours later, reading over their notes one last time, Iris declared, "Yes, I like it."

Meanwhile, Cooper acted as though he hadn't a care in the world as Juliette's troops discussed campaign strategy.

At the VFW, Raymond laughed and danced with his adoring fans as George Strait sang, "And that's why I hang my hat in Tennessee."

Chapter Twenty-Nine

It's Debatable
Campaign strategy

Now that Sarah Hyden-Smith and Iris Long had carved out a platform for Juliette's last-minute mayoral campaign, it was time to talk strategy.

There was no budget for an expensive ad campaign. After all, Juliette's most menacing opponent owned the town's only radio station, and being the ethical journalist she was, Iris couldn't just give Juliette free space in the newspaper.

Fortunately, ministers and editors are generally skilled wordsmiths, and Sarah and Iris knew words could pack a punch. As Iris saw it, their only hope was to engage Cooper and "Silver Tongue" Dick Bland in a public debate.

"Surely," Long said while in deep thought, "there are more people in The Valley like us. It doesn't make sense that we are the only ones who feel the need for another option."

Hyden-Smith agreed. "Most folks have just heard Juliette added her name to the ballot. They have no idea what she stands for. We have to let them know."

Iris concurred. "Let's face it. There have got to be dozens —

maybe hundreds – of voters who feel the same way we do. We need to let them know they have a choice."

"But I've never debated," Juliette interjected. "Do you think my inexperience will make me look foolish against two seasoned speakers? They've been doing this their whole lives."

"You're a smart woman, Juliette," Sarah shot back. "That's what will come through. People will see the difference when you're standing on stage, side by side."

The idea of standing on any stage made Juliette's stomach queasy. She didn't tell her friends, but she was already beginning to feel like she was in over her head.

The group knew getting "Silver Tongue" to debate would be easy. He loved to speak to the masses on stage. Getting Raymond behind a podium, however, would be more difficult. He held a public forum on his show five days a week. Why would he want to risk appearing in front of a group that might be less than hospitable?

It was Juliette's idea to call Raymond the next day, during his Friday *Renderings with Raymond* broadcast, to challenge him publicly. She stayed up half the night, thinking about her call to Raymond.

She would need to trick him into agreeing to a debate. Raymond was no dummy. He knew he was a clear favorite, and debates are generally meant to benefit the underdogs. Her words would be crucial.

Friday marked six days until the election. Caroline's Beauty Salon had its usual crowd, as women of The Valley prepared to look their best for church services on Sunday. All the seats were taken, and hair dryers were humming from every direction.

As usual, the radio played *Renderings with Raymond* while customers sat under hair dryers and in seats along the large window looking out over Bearden's Corner.

At 2:20 precisely, as Vera Penrod was about to say something concerning the evils of Harry Potter, who she had recently begun referring to as "the Devil's son," the room grew silent as Raymond announced, "Let's take another call."

Juliette began her call just as she had prepared, exuding confidence, "Yes, Mr. Cooper. This is Juliette Stoughton, citizen of Lennox Valley."

Obviously surprised, Cooper seemed more amused than concerned by her call. "Is this the same Juliette Stoughton that is allegedly running for mayor of Lennox Valley?"

Expecting that response, Juliette was ready. "Yes, it is. The very same."

"Well, how can I be of service to you today, Juliette?" Cooper said almost coyly. "Do you have a recipe to share, or did you mean to call *Swap Shop*? I'm afraid it doesn't begin until 3:00."

"I would like to challenge you to a debate next Tuesday night," Juliette declared.

"A debate?" Cooper chuckled. "Missy, I know you are new to the complexities of campaigns, but there are only six days left until the election. I'm quite sure this last-ditch effort of yours couldn't even be arranged in such a short period."

Juliette was ready. "Mr. Bland said you would say that. I guess he was right."

"What do you mean by that?" asked an obviously perturbed Cooper.

"I made the same challenge to him this morning. He said he would be happy to debate, but he said you would be afraid to face me on stage. He said you would probably make up some excuse about it being too close to the election date."

"Listen here, missy," Raymond almost shouted into the microphone. "You name the place and time, and I will be there to show you what a real mayor looks like!"

Iris and Sarah both smiled as they sat together by the radio as Juliette answered, "Tuesday night. Seven o'clock. At the Methodist Church. They're donating the use of their fellowship hall."

For a moment, Raymond Cooper was speechless. But just for a moment.

Chapter Thirty

Better Dead
Than red

In just a matter of weeks, the source of the egg price inflation had become public knowledge, Juliette had launched a last-minute campaign for mayor, and the leading candidate had been tricked into agreeing to participate in the town's first public debate since the "Red Menace Debate" back in 1958.

Valley old-timers remembered that spectacle as "Better Dead Than Red" Barry Jarrell faced the incumbent mayor, "Friendly" Wiley Roark.

Both Jarrell and Roark vowed to keep the debate cordial, and it almost worked out that way until Jarrell called the mayor "a Stalin-loving communist from California" 20 seconds into the proceedings. Shortly after, "Friendly" Wiley picked up a metal stand, on loan from the First Baptist Church choir, and smacked it squarely across the jaw of his opponent.

The 1958 debate lasted all of four minutes until fights broke out in the audience. That's when Jarrell roared, "Anyone who would vote for this Red-loving Bolshevik should go on back to Moscow right now!"

No one anticipated as many fireworks in this debate, taking place 40 years later, but it wasn't outside the realm of possibility.

Raymond Cooper began the Monday installment of *Renderings with Raymond* with a quote from Adlai Stevenson, who ran for president against Dwight Eisenhower in 1952. "I offer my opponents a bargain," quoted Cooper. "If they will stop telling lies about me, I will stop telling the truth about them."

The phone rang immediately with restless callers, anxious to chime in during the broadcast.

"Who is this so-called 'Juliette Stoughton'?" Marvin Walsh almost screamed into his phone. "And what makes her think she deserves to share the same stage as Raymond Cooper?"

The next caller, Andy Bowmer, was even more adamant. "Tell her to come by after the debate and clean up," Bowmer jeered. "It seems to me that she should be home cooking dinner for her husband instead of wasting our time."

Cooper, as always, played the role of peacemaker. "Now, listen," he told his audience. "This is America. And every American has the right to run for office, no matter how misguided their efforts might be."

The next caller, Rita Tate, took a different tone. "It seems to me," she said, "we should hear this young woman out. After all, isn't that what America is all about?"

Raymond, not wanting to show disrespect to a potential voter, chimed in. "You're right, Rita," he answered in a charming tone. "Perhaps this is the perfect time to show this young woman, who is new to our community, what Valley hospitality is all about."

Cooper, skillful at manipulating the emotions of his audience, knew this would move the discussion to Juliette's lack of experience in important Valley matters.

What happened next took Raymond by surprise, something that didn't happen very often.

"Hi, Raymond. This is Myrtle Paxley."

"What's on your mind today, Myrtle?" answered the gentle voice of Cooper.

"I just received the strangest call from Springfield. It was somebody taking a poll. They wanted to know who I was going to vote for in the mayor's race. Of course, I told them I was voting for you."

Raymond searched for the right words before saying, "Myrtle, are you sure about that?"

"Yes, I'm sure. They asked if I supported Mayor Bland, you or that new woman. I told them that any real American would vote for you."

Raymond played a commercial for Puckett's Hardware Store while he composed himself.

Following the commercial, Cooper calmly beseeched his listeners, "It is obvious we are facing more than two opponents in the election." After a pause, he continued, "We are facing the mobilized forces of the elite media and the federal government, who will stop at nothing to see this humble American fall."

That afternoon, I was in Springfield, visiting the Rexall Drugstore with my mom when I bumped into "Lightning" Hugh Light as he filled the racks with the latest magazines.

There's something I should tell you about my hometown. Undoubtedly, the two chief forms of entertainment in Lennox Valley in 1998 were politics and church, in no particular order. If we wanted to bowl or play miniature golf, then a trip to Springfield, the county seat, was required.

Professional wrestling came to The Valley a couple of times each year. Most of the wrestlers were from Springfield or some other nearby town, and we'd recognize them if their masks happened to slip. My favorite wrestler was "Lightning" Hugh Light.

I asked why he was putting magazines on the rack, and he told me that was his job. In an instant, professional wrestling lost some of its luster, and it's never been quite the same for me since.

We did, however, have one other form of entertainment in The Valley, The Majestic Theater. With only 1,300 residents, there wasn't enough business to keep a theater open every night, but on Friday and Saturday nights plus Sunday afternoons, the good folks of Lennox Valley could plop down $2 ($1 for children) and spend two hours escaping reality.

With only one screen, movies came and left quickly. Most movies played only one weekend at the Majestic and were replaced with a new title the following week. An exception to that rule was *Saving Private Ryan,* which was in its third week – a record in The Valley – in August 1998.

Callers to *Renderings with Raymond* had come to refer to their hero as "General Cooper," with *Saving Private Ryan* having infiltrated the minds and hearts of Valley residents during the movie's run. Cooper, having never served in the military himself, was happy to take on the honorary mantle.

"I cannot compare to the heroes in that great movie," Raymond would say. "But like them, I've dedicated my life to fighting the forces of evil and destruction right here in our Valley."

Iris felt sick every time she would hear Cooper say something like that, and this election was causing her to feel sick more often than most. With the vote just two days away, and the highly-anticipated mayoral debate only a few hours away, Cooper was in his prime during the Tuesday show and loving every minute of it.

Asked how he felt about a poll being conducted by an unknown organization in Springfield, Raymond reminded the group there were many "outsiders" who hoped to disrupt his campaign, and he was sure this was another ploy by the elite media to steer attention away from the issues.

"Let's face it, the feds are everywhere," he liked to say to his adoring audience. "They are wanting to keep the important matters of this election buried by drumming up fake issues to confuse the voters."

Now that egg prices were no longer discussed on Raymond's show, no one was quite certain to which issues he referred. That didn't seem to matter, however. Whatever these issues were, his faithful fans wouldn't let anything or anyone dilute their enthusiasm.

While most good folks of The Valley were glued to Cooper's show, Iris Long was busy pasting up pages of *The Lennox Valley Hometown News* which would hit the stands the following day. Remember, while computers were becoming commonplace in big-city newsrooms, papers like *The Hometown News* often still laid out pages by hand.

Iris had already decided the main headline would relate to the debate, now only five hours away. She would have a four-column photo of the candidates behind their podiums with the main headline across the top of the page. Underneath the photo, she left plenty of space clear for a cutline and detailed report.

Other than the debate story, Iris left room for only one other piece: an article detailing the results of the just-completed survey of Valley voters. Iris wasn't as young as she once was, and sometimes she found it necessary to stop whatever she was doing and take a breath. This was one of those moments. This was breaking news, and it would be the talk of the town on Wednesday.

While Iris thought about the huge story about to take place, Raymond used the last hour of his Tuesday show to remind listeners to consider their options wisely. He had recently begun referring to Mayor "Silver Tongue" Dick Bland as "Sliver Tongue."

"He is as sneaky as a snake," Cooper liked to say about his rival, "and he is slithering into your homes and wallets, feeling no guilt."

Looking back, I can't help but laugh at Raymond's mutterings concerning Bland, but at the time they struck a chord with his listeners, who made up half of The Valley.

He ended the show by reminding them, "It wouldn't be right for me to use this radio platform to influence your voting decisions."

Then, after a pause, "Just vote your conscience, remembering two of the candidates in the field have no conscience."

Raymond, like Mayor Bland, sure had a way with words. Juliette would need to up her game quickly.

Chapter Thirty-one

Tempers Flare
Prayers become personal

The excitement in The Valley was palpable on Tuesday evening as the good folks made their way to the fellowship hall of the Methodist Church for what would soon be known as "The Debate of the Century."

The atmosphere was similar to that of a county fair or street carnival as Cooper loyalists waved signs proclaiming, "Down with the Federal Reserve!" while the ladies of the Auburn Hat Society passed out lemon cookies to children trying to hang on to their parents along the crowded walkway.

Campaign attire revealed the sentiments of those in the crowd. Raymond Cooper's supporters proudly wore "In Your Heart, You Know He's Right" buttons, while those of "Silver Tongue" Dick Bland's adherents proclaimed "God's Own Man."

Absent from the festivities were any signs of support for Juliette Stoughton, the last-minute candidate who tricked Cooper and Bland into taking part in a debate just two days before the mayoral election. I suppose it was hardly a surprise as only a handful of Valley residents had met Juliette in the year since she moved to town.

Iris Long hurriedly finished laying out Wednesday's issue of *Lennox Valley Hometown News,* leaving only space for a front-page photo and story about the debate. Next to the debate story she listed the results of a just-completed poll of Valley voters under the headline, "Valley Poll Full of Surprises."

Iris left the newspaper office and hurried over to the debate site carrying her well-worn camera and note pad. This election was the biggest story of her long career, and she wasn't about to miss the fireworks that would soon take place at the Methodist Church.

Neither Lennox Valley nor Springfield was big enough for a network-affiliated TV station. However, students at Spring County Community College were on hand to broadcast the debate over the local cable access channel.

Using her influence as secretary of the Spring County Chamber of Commerce, Vera Penrod made arrangements for Matt Pinkin, meteorologist at Channel 6 News, to travel the 60 miles to Lennox Valley to moderate the debate.

All the ingredients were present for a slugfest of historical proportions. The candidates lined the stage in three chairs, with Mayor Dick Bland in the center seat. A single podium graced the stage, blocking those along the center aisle from seeing Bland clearly. A microphone was mounted on the front of the podium and was connected to a portable speaker on the floor below.

Moderator Pinkin took the stage, provoking an almost deafening roar from the audience. Celebrities were rare in The Valley, although 1998 saw more than its share between TV evangelists and performers at the county fair.

As the crowd watched in silence, the coin toss determined who would speak first. Raymond Cooper would be first, followed by Mayor Bland, then Juliette. The moderator told each candidate to make a one-minute opening statement.

Cooper approached the podium as a sizable portion of the audience cheered. Looking over the assembly, he paused, then asked everyone to bow their heads.

As everyone except Iris Long lowered their heads, Raymond began to pray, "Let not the foot of pride come upon me, and let not the hand of the wicked drive me away. There the doers of iniquity have fallen. They have been thrust down and cannot rise."

His fans were beside themselves. Their champion once again was led by God to deliver a heartfelt prayer. That it came straight from Raymond's copy of *Book of Famous Prayers* was unknown to them.

Dick Bland was a seasoned politician. When it was his turn, he also asked the audience to pray with him.

Quoting directly from Judges 15, "Silver Tongue" prayed, "Lord, I have been smitten by the jawbone of an ass."

That's when things began to get out of hand. Cooper supporters took the prayer personally as Bland loyalists cheered the mayor on. It was obvious the meteorologist was in over his head.

Just when it seemed the debate might have ended before it began, the crowd hushed as Juliette Stoughton approached the lectern. Although prayers by Raymond Cooper and Dick Bland incited a near-riot in the Methodist church fellowship hall, voices quickly dulled to whispers as she took her place behind the podium.

As the cacophony quieted, Stoughton took a moment to regain composure before introducing herself.

"Hello. My name is Juliette Stoughton," she began. "I know most of you don't know me, and you are probably wondering what I am doing on this stage with the other candidates for mayor."

"We sure are!" shouted Marvin Walsh to the delight of his fellow Cooper supporters.

Cackles were heard in the VFW section as TV-6 meteorologist Matt Pinkin attempted to take control by reminding the audience the timer would restart at 60 seconds due to the interruption.

That silenced the crowd. No one likes being chastised by a famous celebrity.

Juliette continued. "I'm here," pausing to catch her breath, "because I remember all the wonderful stories I was told about this place."

You could have heard a pin drop as the audience absorbed those simple words.

"I heard about this Valley, filled with wonderful people. I was told they were hard-working, friendly, gentle people. I couldn't wait to see this place and meet these people for myself. I was excited because this Valley would be my home."

Murmuring could be heard among the crowd. "That's right," someone uttered, just loud enough to be made out among the audience.

"Imagine my surprise when the first voice I heard was a voice on the radio." Juliette thought it best to exclude her previous soulmate from her early impressions of The Valley. After all, Chris Roadhouse wasn't even a Valley resident anymore.

The spectators were on the edges of their seats as everyone, even the children, knew Stoughton was referring to Raymond Cooper, host of *Renderings with Raymond* and candidate for mayor of Lennox Valley. Payback would be swift and sure, they were certain.

"This voice was neither gentle nor kind," she continued. "It was mean and hateful, and it made me wonder where the wonderful people I had heard so much about were hiding."

Elbert Lee Jones had heard enough. He was about to shout something, probably neither gentle nor kind, but was subdued by his fellow Cooper supporters who realized Juliette would get a fresh 60 seconds if she was interrupted again.

"I am here," she said quietly, "because I want the Lennox Valley I dreamed of, the Lennox Valley made up of hard-working, friendly neighbors. I want to work toward making our Valley a better place for everyone."

Matt Pinkin reminded Juliette she had 10 seconds remaining on the timer. Extra time wouldn't be an issue when the other candidates returned to the podium.

That's when Juliette responded, "I want a town concerned about real problems, not make-believe issues like rising egg prices and the Federal Reserve."

For a brief moment, you could have heard a pin drop. The room was silent. That's when Rhonda Goodman rose from her seat and began applauding. Her husband, Earl, the mailman and the first to suggest on *Renderings with Raymond* that Cooper should run for office, turned to his wife with a stunned look on his face.

Other women in the audience began to stand and applaud. After a few seconds, there were a dozen or more women, plus a couple of men, rising to their feet and clapping with Rhonda. The rest of the audience remained seated, stunned.

The main headline on the front of *Lennox Valley Hometown News* the next morning read "Newcomer Turns Heads," with the subhead, "Sharp criticism of fake issues incites crowd."

Iris knew how to get the attention of readers, and this headline would surely get its share.

Two photos graced page one. The dominant photo, underneath the headline, showed all three candidates on stage during the coin-flip to determine who would speak first. Raymond grinned. Bland looked irritated, and Juliette watched with her hands folded. A little further down was a picture of Elbert Lee Jones rushing the stage, being held back by Marvin Walsh and two other Cooper supporters.

The only other story on page one included the results of a poll conducted by the Spring County League of Women Voters, which coincidentally included no members of the Lennox Valley Auburn Hat Society:

- Mayor Dick Bland: 30 percent

- Raymond Cooper: 39 percent

- Juliette Stoughton: 3 percent

- Undecided: 28 percent

Being the day before the "Election of the Century," Lennox Valley was captivated by the series of events that had transpired the previous night. *The Hometown News* front page photo of Elbert Lee Jones trying to rush the stage summed up the evening pretty well.

The results of the poll indicated Raymond Cooper's coronation wasn't as sure as many had thought.

Raymond still held a significant lead with 39 percent support in the poll. Current Mayor "Silver Tongue" Dick Bland was nine points behind. It was that undecided vote which had Cooper concerned.

Without Stoughton, he would easily pick up enough undecided votes to reach a majority, but Juliette's entrance into the race changed things.

Cooper wasn't concerned about Juliette beating him. It was obvious she wouldn't be one of two candidates in a run-off, assuming things went that far. She could, however, force the race to continue for another week, subjecting Raymond to another week of campaigning while he watched his lead decline with each passing day.

It would take more than a last-minute entry into the race to frighten Raymond Cooper. He always had a plan.

Cooper began his show with the usual rendition of "Proud To Be An American," followed by a prayer taken verbatim from his *Book of Famous Prayers*. It was an especially powerful prayer to kick off the Wednesday show, including some words from Psalm 109:

They surround me and say hateful things.
They attack me for no reason.
They repay my love with accusations,
but I continue to pray.

In a late night meeting with his "advisers," Marvin Walsh and Farley Puckett, who would serve as Raymond's guests on Wednesday's show, Cooper came up with his plan.

"Issues!" shouted Raymond. "We need more issues."

The trio whittled down a list of a dozen or so compelling issues to three. On Wednesday's show, Raymond didn't waste any time bringing those issues to light.

"Dick Bland has run this city through fear and intimidation for too long," Raymond shouted into the microphone. "That is going to stop when I am mayor. Just like everyone has a voice on this show, every citizen of Lennox Valley will finally have a voice in government when I am mayor."

Rhonda Goodman was in a stylist's chair at Caroline's Beauty Salon when Juliette Stoughton, candidate for mayor, walked in. Juliette was carrying a stack of fliers and asked Caroline if she could put one in her front window that looked out over Bearden's Corner. Caroline told her to hang as many in the window as she wanted.

Juliette seemed relieved. "I haven't had much luck. Most folks won't let me put them in their windows. They always say they have a policy against political fliers, even though they usually have one of Raymond Cooper or Dick Bland on display."

Rhonda asked to see the flier, then read the words aloud: "Mayoral Candidate Juliette Stoughton will appear on Bearden's Corner today at 4:00 to share her vision for Lennox Valley with the public."

At that very moment, *Renderings with Raymond* was back on the air after a commercial break for Massengale's Mortuary. All three ladies paused to hear how Raymond would begin his second hour.

Before Cooper could do more than welcome listeners back, Farley chimed in, "It's hard for me to believe," his volume rising, "that anyone would vote for that woman."

Cooper responded, "She'll get a few votes. She's probably made a few friends in town, and women might be quicker to fall for her nonsense."

"I suppose you're right, as usual," answered Puckett. "Thank goodness most of our Valley women aren't stupid enough to vote for her."

"Dick Bland has been a barefaced puppet of the elite media for too long!" shouted Cooper. "It's pure and simple socialism." He continued, "And a vote for that woman is a shameless wasted vote!"

"I'll be there at four," Rhonda told Juliette after catching her breath.

Caroline chimed in, "Me, too. Can I have a few of those fliers?"

Chapter Thirty-two

Election Day
Sleeping single in a double bed

Election Day finally arrived. Thursday, August 20, 1998, was perhaps the most awaited date in Lennox Valley history. In a year filled with anticipation, featuring visits from celebrities of all types, the mayoral race between current mayor, Dick Bland, and his opponent, Raymond Cooper, had created a greater stir than any event in the 148-year history of The Valley.

Who would have thought an election could draw more attention than Todd Cecil, celebrity evangelist from Branson, Missouri, or an appearance at the upcoming Spring County Fair by Tangi Blevins & the Heavenly Hosts? Perhaps the only event to rival this campaign was the appearance of the first female pastor in The Valley just two months earlier.

Knowing the majority of ballots were entered near the end of the day, Cooper wasted no time in swaying any fence-sitting voters. Raymond began his daily show, *Renderings with Raymond*, three hours early, at 9:00 a.m., under the guise of informing the public of any breaking news on Election Day.

The morning buzz at Caroline's Beauty Parlor focused on one topic: Juliette Stoughton's campaign rally on the square just 18 hours earlier. With the help of Rhonda Goodman and Caroline (who were both persuaded to attend the rally after hearing Stoughton supporters referred to as "stupid" on Cooper's Wednesday show), along with Jessie Orr, waitress at the Hoffbrau, more than 120 women – plus a handful of men – showed up to hear Stoughton speak. You might remember it was Jessie who originally planted the idea of running for office in Juliette's mind as she sipped tea at "the 'Brau" just a few weeks earlier.

As customers discussed the rally, *Renderings with Raymond* could be heard playing on Caroline's speakers.

Realizing Farley Puckett's "stupid" comment might have hurt his standing among female voters, Cooper attempted to heal any wounds by tending to the sensibilities of women listeners.

"I believe a woman has just as much right to run for mayor as anyone else," Raymond muttered as he began hour two of his "special edition." "However," he continued, "it's obvious that a vote for 'Stout-on,'" purposely mispronouncing Juliette's name, "is a wasted vote in this race."

"What kind of name is 'Stouton' anyway?" interrupted Raymond's guest, Earl Goodman. "It sounds kind of Russian to me."

Unbeknownst to the listeners, Earl and Rhonda Goodman slept separately the previous evening for the first time since her mysterious impetigo attack seven years earlier. Earl could not believe his wife of 32 years had been swayed by that "conniving woman."

Raymond was acutely aware that he needed more than 50 percent of the vote to win the election outright. If Juliette could acquire enough votes, she could force a run-off between him and Bland. Even though Cooper had a substantial lead in the Spring County League of Women Voters poll, he could feel his support shrinking with each passing day.

The poll showed him with 39 percent of the voters on his side. If he could draw just half of the 28 percent who declared themselves "undecided," he would win the election handily.

"If she were to get just a few votes," continued Raymond, "she could force a run-off between me and 'Sliver Tongue,'" purposely twisting Bland's nickname. "And even though I would defeat the so-called 'mayor' easily, it seems like a huge waste of taxpayer time and money to hold another election next week."

"Just think of all the things that money could be spent on besides an election," Earl chimed in.

"That's right," said Cooper. "I'd hate to think of all the extra taxes our voters would have to pay to stroke the ego of one self-centered woman."

"The women of our city need to talk to their husbands. Voting against them is like wasting both of their votes," shouted Goodman.

"You know, Earl," offered Raymond, "after dealing with our corrupt Valley government for years, I believe you are the only public servant we have that makes any sense," referring to Goodman's role as mail carrier to the good folks of Lennox Valley.

Several listeners thought they heard a sniffle as Earl whispered, "Thank you, Mr. Mayor."

The Johnson City (Tennessee) Press was one of the first daily newspapers to run The Good Folks of Lennox Valley in 2015. The story still runs today, as evidenced in this April, 2017 issue of The Press.

Chapter Thirty-three

Last Man Standing
Raymond takes no prisoners

In all my days growing up in Lennox Valley, I can't remember a day as tense as Thursday, August 20, 1998. Old-timers still say the tension could match any moment in Valley history, before or since.

As Raymond began hour six of the special edition of his daily show, *Renderings with Raymond*, listeners continued to hang on his every word. One caller after another praised Cooper's leadership as he stood up to the elite media and government authorities who blocked his way along every path.

Raymond had been hinting all day there would be a special surprise during the sixth hour of the show, as he welcomed a different guest at the top of each hour. Guests had already included Farley Puckett, owner of the local hardware store; Earl Goodman, postal carrier and the first to "nominate" Raymond for the mayor's office; Vera Penrod, president of the Auburn Hat Society; Brother Jacob, who left quickly after explaining to Raymond that something had suddenly come up five minutes into his appearance when Cooper took his hand, asking the young associate pastor to pray a prayer of victory; and Worley Fain, chaplain of the Lennox Valley VFW.

Raymond asked Chaplain Fain to prepare a prayer in advance, suggesting he might use one Cooper had penned himself, but actually came from his bedside *Book of Famous Prayers*.

"Dear Lord," began Worley, "You know our struggle is not against flesh and blood, but against the government authorities, against the powers that be, against the forces of darkness, and against the spiritual forces of wickedness that surround us."

Father O'Reilly and Lars Svendsen, senior pastor of Lennox Valley Lutheran Church, made a habit of having a late lunch every Thursday afternoon at the Hoffbrau. As they dined on Reuben sandwiches and sauerkraut, each sipped on his favorite brand of lite beer.

As did most businesses in The Valley, the 'Brau played *Renderings with Raymond* on the sound system as diners enjoyed their meals. As Chaplain Fain began his prayer, the clergymen almost spit beer from their mouths as they recognized the words from Ephesians, Chapter 6.

The men admitted to each other they hadn't been to the voting booth yet. Lennox residents were divided into two precincts. Residents who lived within the "town" precinct voted in the fellowship hall of First Baptist Church. Raymond had mentioned on several occasions the location held an unfair advantage for Mayor Bland, who was a member there.

Folks who lived in the "country" precinct voted at the VFW, located on Highway 11. Cooper never seemed to notice the same could be said about the polling location of the country precinct. You would be hard pressed to find a VFW member who wasn't solidly in Raymond's corner.

As was often the case, the two veteran clergymen took their time, enjoying the solace of conversation between close friends.

Jessie, waitress at the 'Brau for longer than anyone could remember, quizzed her customers. "Who do you think the surprise guest will be, padres?"

154

She called all the local clergymen "padre," except Brother Billy Joe Prather, who took exception to the colloquial tone. She had yet to settle on a nickname for Sarah Hyden-Smith.

"It's not me," quipped Father O'Reilly.

"Me, neither," added Pastor Svendsen, "although my shadow," sarcastically referring to Brother Jacob, "took advantage of the limelight for a brief moment this morning."

The three hushed as Raymond began hour six of his show.

"Our guest for this hour needs no introduction," Raymond began. "I have on the phone none other than Dean Morris, who starred as Deke McClellan in 'Don't Shoot Nellie!' which is quite possibly the most memorable first-season episode of *Walker, Texas Ranger*."

"Good Lord," sighed Father O'Reilly.

"It sounds like you're doing mighty important work in Leonard Valley," began Morris. "Those folks are sure lucky to have you on their side."

Cooper responded with words that seemed totally authentic to his listeners, "I'm humbled."

The part-time celebrity was on and gone within three minutes, but Raymond Cooper was certain Dean Morris had just put him over the top.

TIMES NEWS

Missouri Valley

MISSOURI VALLEY   NEWS   SPORTS   OBITS   LIVING   OPINION   COMMUNITY   PUBLIC NOT

The Good Folks of Lennox Valley

By Kevin Slimp   Apr 19, 2017   💬 0

The barber shop knew – new shop rivals 'Bras for inside scoop

Being a barber is a lot like being a priest, or even a bartender. Customers might tell you anything; a funny story, a lesson in town history, or even their deepest, darkest secrets. It is an almost sacred calling.

There's something about sitting in a barber's chair that seems oddly familiar. For many, climbing on the booster seat is one of our earliest childhood memories. The sound of clippers and the feel of the brush on the back of your neck conjures recollections of a bygone era.

When the barber clips the black vinyl drape around your neck, it's almost impossible for your mind to keep from wandering back in years long gone.

Frank Bell opened his shop on Main Street less than two weeks earlier, yet in that time he had learned enough about the good folks of Lennox Valley to fill a couple of novels had he been a writer. After living most of his life in the "big city" of Terre Haute, Indiana, Frank was starting to find 'that he knew more intimate details of The Valley after two weeks than he learned about his former home in 38 years.

Between his new church, news from the strangers who hung out in the shop after school and his visit two days earlier with Sarah, pastor of the Methodist Church, Frank was becoming somewhat of an authority on town history. It wouldn't be long before he would be as confused as everyone else concerning the seemingly constant drama surrounding his new home.

The Missouri Valley (Iowa) TimesNews runs The Good Folks of Lennox Valley each week.

Chapter Thirty-Four

Counting the Votes

Cheers, jeers and fears

On a riser at the front of the room sat a large white board with the names Bland, Cooper and Stoughton across the top. A fourth column with the word "Other" fit along the right edge. Tallies were recorded by Maxine Miller, who used a large black marker. The atmosphere was as thick as soup.

To begin the process, Vera Penrod shouted, "Cooper!" twice. Maxine recorded two tallies under Raymond's name as the VFW section of the Town Hall, which included 14 members of the local group, cheered in anticipation of the expected landslide victory of their champion.

Cooper, always confident, grinned knowingly. It was a good start for the "Man of the People."

Their cheers came to an almost immediate halt as Vera shouted, "Bland," reading the name on the third ballot. Some in the audience were already expecting a landslide for Raymond.

The anticipation was palpable. Inside the room, 100 lucky lottery winners waited on edge. An overriding tenseness could be felt throughout the room as folks sat on the edge of their seats, waiting for the next name to be called. Outside, speakers had been hastily set up so those not fortunate enough to get inside could hear the proceedings. It wasn't the most comfortable setup for those who didn't win the lottery, but it was better than nothing.

Earlier, just before the vote count began, Vera announced there was a record turnout to mark ballots in the mayoral race. In the previous election, just the usual 800 or so good folks of The Valley turned out to vote. According to the records of the precinct coordinators, a total of 934 voters had marked ballots on this election day. That was all but four of the registered voters in The Valley.

"Cooper!" Vera shouted, followed by cheers from the VFW section.

"Bland!" she continued the count, as Iris Long jotted the vote results on her reporter's note pad. She had drawn two lines down her page to divide the three candidates' votes. So far, Juliette's column was empty.

After five minutes of tallying, the board indicated 24 votes for Raymond Cooper, 19 votes for "Silver Tongue" Dick Bland, and no votes for Juliette Stoughton.

Raymond began to breathe more easily as his concern that Juliette's last minute entrance might harm his chances of getting a majority of the votes, which was needed to win the mayor's race outright, dwindled away. She seemed less of a threat by the minute.

Finally, at the 5:07 mark, Vera shouted, "Mickey Mouse!" and the crowd broke out in laughter. Mickey, along with Ima Goose, Ronald Reagan and a few others, generally received a dozen or more votes, but wasted ballots were much less common during the 1998 race. It was obvious one vote could make a difference, and most folks wanted to be sure their votes counted.

The laughter subsided as Vera announced the name on ballot number 45, "Juliette Stoughton!"

There were no boos or cheers, as had been the case every time

Cooper or Bland received a vote. There was just an audible sigh emanating throughout the room.

Finally, Marvin Walsh, watching from the corner of the room, shouted, "I guess she had to vote for herself!" as several folks inside Town Hall and outside on the front steps laughed in response.

Not everyone laughed, however. Outside, Earl Goodman's laugh quickly subsided as his wife Rhonda, who was sleeping separately from him for only the second time in their marriage, glared at him with a look that sent chills up his spine.

"Stoughton!" shouted Vera, calling out Juliette's name again.

Raymond received the next vote. Then, Mayor Bland, then two votes for Juliette. There was a mumble throughout the Town Hall. The Cooper section was noticeably silent.

At the 51:49 mark, Iris noted half the ballots had been counted. She quickly looked over her note pad as Vera announced a five-minute recess before the tally would continue.

Iris had been very careful as she jotted down the vote count. After 467 votes, the tally looked like this:

Dick Bland: 137

Raymond Cooper: 234

Juliette Stoughton: 91

Mickey Mouse: 2

Ima Goose: 3

Outside, Farley Puckett turned to his wife and said, "How can there be 90 people dumb enough to vote for that woman?"

It didn't take long for Farley to realize his error. From the look on his wife's face, he realized Earl wasn't the only man who would be sleeping alone in The Valley tonight.

Iris counted and recounted the votes during the five-minute recess. It was difficult to concentrate with a room full of Valley residents, all loudly sharing their thoughts concerning the ballot tally.

Half the votes were counted, and Raymond held a considerable lead. With 53 percent of the vote so far, Cooper could win the mayor's race outright if things continued to go his way.

Cooper and his supporters had been worried Juliette Stoughton's late entry into the race might hurt his chances of collecting more than 50 percent of the votes, a necessity to avoid a run-off with the obvious second choice, Dick Bland. There was concern Bland might fare better with another week to campaign. Thankfully, it looked like Cooper's tactics had worked, and enough voters were frantic about the Federal Reserve System to carry their champion to victory.

Juliette had already surprised everyone by collecting 19 percent of the vote thus far. Though still far behind Bland, who was selected on 29 percent of the ballots, she had no reason to be ashamed. Apparently Cooper had angered enough of the electorate to throw 91 voters her way.

As the last chorus of "One Day at a Time" blared from the boom box on stage, Vera Penrod brought the room to a hush as she roared, "Stoughton!" A tally was placed under Juliette's name on the board.

A few Cooper supporters hissed, then giggled, to indicate their lack of concern. Their candidate needed only 47 percent of the remaining votes. Surely, Juliette had received most of her votes already, and their man would win in a landslide.

Outside, where hundreds of good folks gathered to listen to the proceedings over speakers in front of the Town Hall, a voice shouted, "Yes! Way to go, Juliette!"

It was none other than Jessie, the waitress at the 'Brau, who originally suggested Juliette should place her name on the ballot. The crowd outside quieted for a moment, realizing Juliette obviously had at least one vocal supporter.

"Cooper!" shouted Vera. Then, "Stoughton!"

More cheers, mostly from females, erupted from outside.

"Cooper!" Vera roared.

"Stoughton," she continued. "And another vote for Stoughton!"

Twelve more votes were tallied before Vera finally shouted, "Bland!"

There was a murmur throughout the room. Iris looked at her count. Still far behind Mayor Bland, Juliette was showing momentum, and the room was filled with speculation.

"Cooper! Stoughton! Stoughton! Bland! Stoughton! Cooper!" Vera shouted the votes purposely as the count reached the 90-minute mark. There was a definite buzz in the room as folks looked on in astonishment.

Iris continued tallying votes on her reporter's pad, but she gave up trying to keep up with the count as Vera called out names almost faster than Iris could mark them on the page.

Finally, like a runner sprinting to the finish line, Vera read the names on the final stack of ballots.

"Cooper!" she shouted. Next she yelled, "Bland!" creating a stir from the Baptist section of the room, eerily silent since the mid-count break.

"Stoughton!" Vera drew a deep breath. "And the final vote is for Juliette Stoughton!"

Farley Puckett was beside himself as he looked over to see his wife cheering along with other women gathered outside the Town Hall. He started to say something to her, but thought the better of it, remembering how uncomfortable his living room sofa was.

Iris went over her notes as most of the crowd inside the hall attempted to tally the votes in their heads. She could hardly believe what she was seeing on her pad.

Chief of Police Buford Dibble eyed the crowd carefully, looking for any signs of a potential riot while Vera and the two precinct coordinators scratched their chins as they peered at the tally board and looked over their notes several times.

The crowd silenced as Vera approached the microphone. She took a deep breath before she began. It was obvious the intensity of the vote count had taken its toll.

"The final vote is as follows," Vera began. "Dick Bland: 229 votes."

The crowd took a collective breath.

"Raymond Cooper: 466 votes."

A murmur turned into conversations before Chief Dibble quieted the audience.

"Juliette Stoughton: 231 votes."

"Mickey Mouse, Ima Goose and Ronald Reagan had eight votes between them."

"Oh, my!" Iris whispered as she double-checked her figures. She had been right. Juliette really did outpace Mayor Bland by two votes.

Beatrice Justice, overhearing Iris, turned to her and said, "Ecclesiastes 1, verse 2."

It took a few moments for the results to sink in, but eventually bedlam erupted in the Town Hall following the mayoral vote count.

Iris Long, editor of *Lennox Valley Hometown News*, checked and rechecked her figures against those on the board. Vera Penrod and the others on stage frantically clicked the keys on their calculators, making sure they didn't miss any votes.

When Chief Dibble walked to the microphone, you could have heard a pin drop in the room. Dibble always dressed in a dark olive uniform when on duty, the kind that made him look even more intimidating. It was obvious he meant business on this night.

"Election Coordinator Penrod has an announcement concerning the vote," Dibble barked. "We must have complete order in the room. I repeat, we will maintain order. We will not stand for any disorderly outbursts."

No one was sure who "we" were, since Chief Dibble was the

only police officer in Lennox Valley. The crowd acquiesced, just the same. No one wanted on the Chief's bad side. They remembered what happened when A.J. Fryerson got on Dibble's bad side.

Vera began, "We have counted and recounted the votes. The numbers we reported a few minutes ago are correct. Raymond Cooper received 466 votes."

Shouts of "Yes!" were heard from the Cooper section of the room. Order was quickly restored when Chief Dibble glared directly at Marvin Walsh, the primary culprit.

"Mayor Bland," Vera continued, "received 229 votes, and Juliette Stoughton received a total of 231 votes."

An audible murmur began to rise throughout the hall but quickly dissipated as Vera spoke again.

"Counting the eight votes cast for write-ins, we have a total of 934 votes. The leading vote-getter, Raymond Cooper, received 466 votes."

The Cooper corner erupted in a chorus, led by Marvin Walsh, of "Mayor Cooper, Mayor Cooper, Mayor Cooper!"

A hard look from Chief Dibble restored order as Vera continued. "We've calculated the votes four times, and the result is the same each time. Raymond Cooper is two votes shy of a majority. We will conduct a run-off election between Raymond Cooper and Juliette Stoughton, who received two more votes than Mayor Bland, one week from today."

Shouts began to erupt throughout the Town Hall. A voice was heard from the back of the room, "It's a fix!"

Iris Long took pictures of the melee following the announcement. Rhonda Goodman, standing outside with the majority of folks who weren't selected to watch the election festivities inside, listened to the proceedings over the speakers on the Town Hall steps. It was then she heard a familiar voice from inside the hall.

There was no doubt about it. It was her husband, Earl, yelling, "It's a sham! You are puppets of the Federal Reserve System! This

163

will not stand! This will not stand!"

Marvin Walsh joined in the fracas by rushing to the edge of the stage and shouting at the election coordinators. "We want a recount! You are tools of the federal government! We demand a recount!"

Within seconds, the door to the Town Hall opened, and Chief Dibble exited the building behind Marvin Walsh and Earl Goodman, who were handcuffed to each other. Iris Long followed, taking pictures as quickly as she could focus her trusty Nikon, as the men made their way to the police station across the square.

Over the noise of the crowd, Father O'Reilly barely heard the voice of Brother Billy Joe Prather over the speakers. Apparently, he was trying to restore order by asking the room to bow in prayer. Unfortunately for Brother Prather, it sounded like there weren't many folks in the mood to pray at the moment.

Just then, the doors to the Town Hall opened again. As the crowd watched, Raymond Cooper emerged. Several in the crowd began to chant, "Cooper, Cooper, Cooper!"

Raymond stood there appreciatively, finally quieting the crowd by motioning with his hands.

"Friends. I know that many of you think what happened tonight was a travesty of justice. I must admit, I have my doubts about what just took place in there. But this is America, and we have no choice but to abide by the wishes of the election coordinators."

Much of the crowd began shouting, "No! No! No!" until Raymond continued.

"I've asked Worley Fain, chaplain of our Valley VFW, to lead us in prayer."

"Good Lord," Jessie, waitress at the Hoffbrau, muttered just loud enough for Cooper to hear.

"That's the spirit!" shouted Cooper. "Do you hear that, Chaplain? They're starting without you."

Chapter Thirty-Five

The Perfect Scheme
Faith Hill inspires underdog

When the good folks of Lennox Valley began to stir on Friday morning, many wondered if the events of Thursday evening had been a dream. Let's face it – most of the previous six months seemed like a nightmare, so why should election night have been any different?

As coffee began brewing and phones began ringing, it was soon apparent Thursday night had not been a dream, and there were more questions than there had been just 24 hours earlier.

Did Juliette Stoughton really keep Raymond Cooper from winning the election outright, forcing a run-off? Did Earl Goodman and Marvin Walsh really get arrested for disturbing the peace after rushing the stage following the mayoral election count while shouting at the election officials? Did anyone bail Goodman and Walsh out, or were they still sitting in the lone Lennox Valley jail cell?

Iris Long slept less than three hours, working past midnight in an unsuccessful attempt to get interviews with all three candidates. She also attempted to interview Chief Dibble, but he would have none of it. He had just prevented a riot from overtaking our peaceful Valley, arresting two of the town's leading citizens in the process.

The Hoffbrau opened at 6:30 a.m. for breakfast, and Iris was there when Sarah Hyden-Smith and Juliette Stoughton arrived at 6:35. All three were exhausted from the events of the previous evening, but none as tired as Iris. She was, after all, older than both her cohorts combined.

The run-off was a mere six days away. While it seemed reasonable to assume Stoughton could keep her voters, it was absurd to imagine all of "Silver Tongue" Dick Bland's supporters coming over to her side. Plus, there were the eight votes for Mickey Mouse, Ima Goose and Ronald Reagan with which to contend.

Other than the noon to 3:00 p.m. time slot, the 'Brau played music from the "three towers of country power" in Springfield. Jessie, 'Brau waitress, couldn't tolerate Raymond Cooper more than three hours each day, even if his voice was only heard during commercial breaks and during *Swap Shop* outside of his *Renderings with Raymond* time slot.

As they contemplated Juliette's next move, they could hear Mark Chesnutt singing in the background, "It's a little too late."

It was then Jessie pulled up a chair from the adjoining table and placed it at the end of the trio's booth. Jessie was, after all, the first person to suggest Juliette run for office, so she felt she had a right to be a part of the election team.

"You know," Jessie began, "I wasn't always a waitress. I've been a business owner, just like you, Iris."

Juliette and her friends sipped coffee as they listened respectfully.

"I used to own the diner on Highway 11."

Iris, who had been editor of *The Hometown News* for as long as anyone could remember, spoke up. "That's right. I had forgotten that. It was so long ago."

"Yes, 27 years to be exact," offered Jessie.

166

"What happened?" asked Sarah.

"I had three children and a husband back then. I realized I could either own a diner, or I could raise my kids and be happy, but I couldn't do all three."

"But don't you regret giving that up?" Juliette asked. "Do you ever wish you had kept your diner?"

"Well," Jessie paused for a moment before continuing, "I realized some people are born to run businesses, and some people just don't have the stomach for it. That was me. I was pretty good at it, but it wasn't so good for me."

"What are you trying to say, Jessie?" Iris inquired. "That Juliette doesn't have the stomach to be mayor? That she should just give up and let Raymond Cooper win?"

"I'm not trying to say anything," Jessie offered with her local drawl. "I'm just telling a story. That's all."

At that moment, another song began playing. There was quiet in the Hoffbrau as the singer sang, "Waking up in someone else's dream."

"Faith Hill," noted Jessie, "seems like the happiest person in the world. But when she sings a song like that, you realize it hasn't always been easy for her."

With that, the group stopped talking and listened as Faith finished her song. Juliette realized for much of her life, she had been living someone else's dream. She also knew those days were past. Chris Roadhouse was gone. She would someday realize she was a lot better off without him. But those things take time.

"It's going to sound crazy," Juliette said, "but I know what I'm going to do.

Two days earlier, it was assumed by just about everyone in Lennox Valley that attention would turn on Friday morning from the mayor's race to the upcoming county fair.

However, as word swiftly spread across The Valley that Juliette

167

Stoughton was holding a rally on the town square at 6:00 p.m., folks wondered just what her campaign strategy was going to be. There would surely be a crowd.

Shortly after their early morning meeting with Iris Long at the Hoffbrau, Sarah Hyden-Smith and Juliette could be seen rushing to *The Hometown News* office. Soon after, they were seen leaving just as quickly, carrying leaflets.

The leaflet, printed with black ink on green paper, included large bold letters across the top spelling:

ATTENTION, Juliette Stoughton SUPPORTERS!

Below were the words:

Rally at 6:00 p.m. on the town square

In smaller letters near the bottom of the page was the admonition, "Please spread the word! Tell your friends and family members!"

No one was surprised by the primary topic of conversation on *Renderings with Raymond* that Friday afternoon. Before discussing Juliette's rally, however, there were a few other matters to cover. Raymond told the audience the show might go past its usual three hours.

Both Earl Goodman and Marvin Walsh were on hand. One caller after another praised their heroism and patriotism for having been arrested in defense of their fearless leader, Raymond Cooper. Both described their precarious evening at the mercy of Chief Dibble. Having been locked in a cold, damp jail cell, they each described fearing they would not live to see the light of day.

"Dibble is a puppet of the elite media!" Walsh shouted into the microphone.

"He is obviously on the payroll of Juliette Stoughton and her minions," countered Goodman, not sure what a "minion" really was. "And besides, from my cell I saw him make at least two long-distance calls. I could only assume he was calling his superiors in Washington for instructions."

It was obvious, Walsh and Goodman had temporarily forgotten the unwritten code concerning getting on Chief Dibble's bad side. They would be reminded of it soon enough.

At Caroline's Beauty Salon, patrons sat patiently as Raymond and his crew could be heard ganging up on local officials. Friday was the busiest day of the week as customers prepared to look their best for Sunday services. Hair dryers were buzzing and magazine pages were flipping as Raymond spoke.

"I'm starting to think I never should have voted for that Raymond Cooper," declared Diane Norris as she listened to him ridicule his political opponents and anyone who agreed with them.

"Marvin Walsh always was a blow-hard," observed Heather Blake.

One by one, Caroline's patrons expressed dismay at ever thinking Raymond Cooper would make a good mayor. It was like they had been hanging onto Cooper's words by a delicate thread which was becoming more frayed.

Meanwhile, Raymond was in his glory, discussing his future regime. The corruption of the past would be gone. The reign of terror led by "Silver Tongue" Dick Bland was near its end. The totalitarian rule, beholden to federal agencies, was almost a thing of the past. Peace and prosperity were at hand, and Cooper would lead his listeners to the Promised Land.

And what about Juliette Stoughton and her 6:00 p.m. rally on the town square?

"It's just another attempt to make a name for herself," Cooper barked to the cheers of his studio guests. "Let her have her fun. It won't last much longer."

By 5:30 p.m., the doors to most of The Valley's shops were locked. Caroline, cleaning up her shop, could see a crowd, mostly women, gathering on the square. Soon, however, Caroline noticed a few men arriving, obviously trying to see what this mischief-maker had up her sleeve.

At 6:05, more than half The Valley was assembled in front of the steps to the Town Hall. A hush came over the crowd as Juliette walked to the top step and addressed the audience.

"Citizens of Lennox Valley," she began. "Thank you for taking the time to be here this afternoon."

"Anything for our next mayor!" came a shout from the back of the crowd. It was Jessie.

This brought more shouts and applause from those gathered before Juliette continued, "I have a plan, and I think it might work."

The crowd of Stoughton supporters hushed, waiting to hear what their hero had in mind.

Chapter Thirty-Six

Raymond Concerned
Celebrity adds her voice

The special edition of *Renderings with Raymond* took The Valley by surprise Monday morning. Most folks expected fireworks on the first show following Juliette Stoughton's huge announcement on Friday, but even his most loyal followers didn't expect their champion to begin three hours earlier than usual.

If Raymond had his way, he would have started his show at sunup, but Marvin and Earl convinced him too many folks would miss his opening dialog if he began that early.

Following a rousing rendition of "The Star Spangled Banner," recorded in 1983 by Tangi Blevins & the Heavenly Hosts, Raymond introduced Lutheran pastor Brother Jacob, who reluctantly offered a prayer to begin the show. Inviting Brother Jacob was a tactical maneuver meant to sway any "fence-sitting" Lutheran run-off voters to move into the Cooper camp before the Thursday vote.

Cooper thanked the young pastor, then added, "Surely the Lord is on our side," turning down Jacob's microphone before the young minister had a chance to respond.

It had been a harried three days for much of The Valley as folks discussed the surprise announcement by mayoral candidate Juliette Stoughton on Friday evening. Citing a little-known passage in the Lennox Valley Election Code written in 1948, Juliette withdrew from the run-off election within 24 hours of the Thursday ballot count, allowing "Silver Tongue" Mayor Dick Bland to slide into her spot and run head-to-head against Raymond Cooper six days later.

"I cannot believe," shouted Cooper as he began his show, "that woman thinks the good folks of Lennox Valley are naive enough to follow her orders and cast their votes for our alleged 'mayor' of the past four years!"

The phone lights were already blinking. Raymond had increased his phone lines from one to four during the campaign season to accommodate the increased traffic of callers. Marvin Walsh and Farley Puckett were helping out by manning the phones. They could have used several more helpers.

Although the youth were busy preparing their prized lambs and rabbits for the Spring County Fair set to begin the next day, and Valley women were testing their recipes one final time, the drama surrounding the upcoming vote kept most listeners glued to their radios. Just about everyone in The Valley was tuned into *Renderings with Raymond* that morning.

Cooper was concerned. History is filled with politicians who kicked off loud, boisterous campaigns filled with grand ideas. Like many such campaigns, he had attracted a loyal following. As is often the case, however, the more time passed, the more folks began to realize Raymond's platform was made up of make-believe issues and empty promises.

Realizing she had no chance to overtake Cooper in a run-off election, Juliette asked all her supporters to cast their ballots for Bland. She made a special plea to those who had voted for Mickey Mouse, Ima Goose and Ronald Reagan.

"We need your votes to count," she shared. "Every last one of your votes is crucial."

Cooper recited a laundry list of "powers and principalities" who were conspiring to take what was rightfully his. They included Iris Long and the rest of the elite media; the Federal Reserve System; Chief Dibble and his friends in Washington; Sarah Hyden-Smith, a newcomer who had come to town with her hyphenated name and dangerous new ideas; and Juliette Stoughton with her political machine.

He had a surprise of his own, however. Waiting on the line to speak with Raymond was none other than Tangi Blevins, who hadn't heard the tirade preceding their conversation. She had simply volunteered to be interviewed on the show, thinking they would be talking about her upcoming performance at the county fair. As was often the case, Raymond had a way of surprising folks.

Raymond praised the gospel-singing celebrity scheduled to perform at the fair on Friday night, telling her how much he loved her song, "Turn Your Radio On." A few more moments of artificial flattery was followed with a question, "May I ask you something personal, Tangi?"

Her initial thought was, "That depends on what it is." But Raymond knew better than to give her a chance to answer.

Without pausing, he continued. "Given the choice, would you vote for a puppet of the wealthy elite, hand-picked by the media and federal government," pausing momentarily, "or would you vote for a God-fearing, humble servant of the people?"

"If those were my only choices, I suppose I'd vote for the humble servant of the people."

Quickly thanking Tangi before hanging up the phone, Raymond leaned into the microphone and softly said, "There you have it. Right from the mouth of America's biggest gospel celebrity."

Leaning over Cooper's shoulder, toward the microphone, Marvin added, "I believe that's our first endorsement of the day, Mayor!"

Sitting by the radio in her rocker, Beatrice Justice whispered knowingly, "Proverbs 16, verse 18."

Listening in her office, Iris Long whispered, "That scoundrel."

Chapter Thirty-seven

Fair Election
Even the pigs are panicked

Mary Ann Tinkersley and I had spent months together, walking our lambs in anticipation of the FFA judging at the upcoming Spring County Fair. My lamb, Archibald, was looking fit. Mary Ann's entry, Snowflake, was in pristine condition by the time August rolled around and was my favorite to win.

It was hard to imagine which was subject to more discussion, the county fair or the election, as Wednesday began. Iris Long, editor of *The Lennox Valley Hometown News*, wrote as much in her weekly editorial.

"Every town," Iris began, "deserves a week each year to take a break from the ordinary. What better way than to watch our youth display their prize-winning animals, ride a Ferris wheel, or see our favorite entertainers in person?"

"This week," she continued, "we will enjoy our fair, but at the same time we have important business at hand." She was, of course, writing about the mayoral election.

"Let me suggest," she wrote, "we face reality and see Raymond Cooper for who he really is."

She went on to detail Cooper's antics, from the egg price-fixing scheme to his "conversion" at the Lutheran church.

"Join me," she continued, "in voting for Dick Bland for mayor of Lennox Valley." She concluded her editorial, "When the election is over Thursday evening, we can all take a collective breath and enjoy our children, our fair and our community in the way they are meant to be enjoyed."

As much as I had prepared for this day, in my heart I wanted Mary Ann to win to blue ribbon. As I sat in my stall trimming the wool on Archibald's legs, I could see Mary Ann brushing Snowflake after bringing her in from a bath. It was important to clean and brush the animals just before the contest.

The livestock were kept in a barn next to the Pavilion, which housed displays from gutter companies, real estate agents and the John Deere dealer from Springfield. The Pavilion was usually relatively quiet, with folks walking through to look at displays and fill out cards, hoping to win a used car, ironing board, or some other valuable prize. Springfield radio stations provided celebrity on-air personalities to add excitement.

The fair gates opened on Wednesday at 11:00 a.m., allowing folks to wander through and look over livestock before competitions began at 2:00 p.m. Generally not much happened before the competitions, but this was no normal year. At noon Mary Ann and I heard what sounded like a commotion coming from the Pavilion. We headed that way with everyone else.

When I got to the Pavilion, I could barely believe my eyes. There was Raymond Cooper, beginning his live broadcast of *Renderings with Raymond* from the Spring County Fair.

As an excited fair-goer handed her baby to the candidate, Raymond pronounced, "You know, I've heard Dick Bland doesn't like babies."

Seated at a table next to the standing Cooper, Marvin Walsh bellowed, "I heard he hates puppies and kittens, too!"

Some say it was an act of God. Others claim it was a political conspiracy. Fair officials blamed it on a faulty latch.

Whatever the cause, it was exactly 12:17 p.m. on Wednesday, August 26, 1998, when no fewer than 11 full-sized, potentially prize-winning pigs escaped Livestock Barn B and stampeded straight toward the entrance to the Spring County Fair Pavilion.

Raymond Cooper, making a surprise live appearance at the fair to host *Renderings with Raymond*, was deeply engrossed in his opening monologue concerning the corruption of "so-called 'Mayor' Dick Bland" and his "dirty" administration.

"I assure you," Raymond shouted into his microphone while dozens of adoring fans looked on, "I am going to stand tall with the good folks of The Valley and clean up the mess that my alleged 'opponent' has created!"

Then, bowing his head, his mouth almost touching the microphone, he continued, "And I want to express my humble gratitude to the Good Lord above, who has bestowed so many blessings upon my candidacy."

The last thing anyone remembered hearing before the ensuing onslaught was Marvin Walsh shouting, "Amen!"

At least one observer later told Iris Long, editor of *The Hometown News*, it reminded her of a rushing flood. Still others compared it to a scene from *Braveheart*, when Mel Gibson, playing the role of William Wallace – a 13th-century Scottish warrior who led the Scots in the First War of Scottish Independence against King Edward – followed by a hoard of screaming warriors, attacked the British army with blazing precision.

Iris Long, on hand to photograph Mayor Bland greeting fair-goers as part of the opening festivities, could barely believe what she was seeing. She seemed to be one of the few in the audience not surprised by Cooper's appearance. It was just the type of thing she had come to expect from him.

In her five decades of journalistic experience, however, nothing had prepared her for what was taking place in front of her eyes.

Suddenly, the crowd began to part like the Red Sea in Old Testament times, away from the path of the oncoming swine. Raymond Cooper could scarcely believe his own eyes. As if in a trance, he stood frozen as the sows moved ever closer.

The swarming pigs seemed to take aim at Raymond, as if guided by some external force. Charging closer still, they moved directly toward Cooper, knocking him to the ground in their stampede. The crowd looked on in shock, no one knowing what to do. Charging swine weren't an everyday occurrence in The Valley.

Not one to let an opportunity such as this escape, Mayor Bland quickly rushed over to Raymond, who was covered in dirt and hoof prints. Extending his hand to lift Cooper from the ground, the mayor paused momentarily, then turned his head toward the shocked onlookers.

"I knew that my opponent was skilled in slinging mud," Bland bellowed, "but I had no idea he was so adept at wallowing in it!"

Iris focused her trusty Nikon at the two men: Cooper, still barely rising off the ground, and Bland, smiling giddily as he lifted Raymond to his feet.

We rarely saw Raymond Cooper dumbstruck in 1998. For a moment, though, those reassembled stood in silence, wondering if their champion was uncharacteristically at a loss for words.

Finally steady on his feet, Raymond spoke words only he could devise at such a moment. "I find it mighty interesting that my opponent just happened to be so close when those pigs were released from their secured pens."

Bland started to respond, but Cooper cut him off.

"I also find it peculiar," looking toward Iris Long, "that the principal representative of the elite media just happens to be here, as well."

Iris could barely believe her ears. He was doing it again. Raymond Cooper was going to convince his supporters this was planned all along by the "powers and principalities" aligned against him. Iris was right. He was a scoundrel.

In spite of my youth, I realized something substantial had just taken place. In one brief moment, Raymond Cooper, adored by many and loathed by others, was transformed from near superhero status to mere flesh and bones. His quick thinking to insinuate blame upon his opponent and the elite media might have placated his most ardent supporters, but for others it was an eye-opening experience.

Could it be Raymond Cooper was not the intellectual giant many of us had assumed? Was Iris Long right all along? Had Cooper created his own reality and manipulated his listeners into believing things that weren't true?

It's amazing how many things can go through a young man's mind at a moment like this. I wanted to get back to Mary Ann and our lambs, as FFA judging was only hours away, but I couldn't help but think something important had just happened. Like most others in the Pavilion, I stood stupefied for what seemed like hours, but was probably only seconds.

By dinner time, most everyone in The Valley was discussing what had already become known as "the great pig panic."

As one might expect, Raymond was more than a little flustered as he attempted to fill the remaining two hours of *Renderings with Raymond*. The afternoon was supposed to have been a celebration of Cooper's many accomplishments but instead became a muddled attempt to explain what had just taken place.

Mayor Bland, manning his own campaign booth less than 50 feet away, told his supporters the episode reminded him of a story in the Bible when Jesus cast a demon into a herd of pigs, who then stampeded to their own deaths.

"I am a simple man, not a theologian," Bland told those gathered, "so I am not suggesting that Raymond Cooper has any affiliation with demonic forces. But it's mighty peculiar the way they focused on him."

Then, after a pause, he added, "I would suggest, however, this discussion might best be held in conjunction with your family and clergyman. I am just a simple servant of the people."

No wonder they called him "Silver Tongue."

None of us had ever seen Raymond so discombobulated. For the next two hours, most of his show was comprised of his most ardent supporters sharing their theories concerning the stampede.

Earl Goodman reported seeing a mysterious figure in what appeared to be a "Stand with Bland" t-shirt near the gate holding the pigs just before the attack. Elbert Lee Jones said it was common knowledge that pig farmers were big fans of Bland.

In bed that evening, I thought about the FFA judging that afternoon. I thought of how pretty Mary Ann Tinkersley looked in her Round House overalls. And I wondered, just wondered, if those pigs – demon-possessed or not – might have ruined Raymond Cooper's chance to be our next mayor.

Chapter Thirty-eight

It's Now or Never

Who will be Valley mayor?

The morning of "The Great Valley Run-off," I listened at the breakfast table as my parents discussed their options while considering how they would cast their votes.

I think my father, who owned the town bookstore by day and repaired TVs in our basement at night, summed up how many good folks of The Valley felt when he said, "I'm not sure it's worth the time it takes to vote."

Raymond began *Renderings with Raymond* in earnest at 7:00 a.m., five hours earlier than usual. He kept saying something about his public duty to keep the town informed, but most folks realized he was trying to gain a few votes in an election that was getting closer by the minute.

"Silver Tongue" Dick Bland held a campaign rally on the town square at 8:00 a.m., hoping to influence any voters sitting on the fence. He kissed Christine Schmidt's baby – noting it was quite possibly the most beautiful baby he had ever seen – and shook hands with the 40 or so folks in attendance, making his final attempt at convincing Juliette Stoughton's adherents to follow her wishes and cast their ballots for him.

You would think the county fair, 11 miles away toward Springfield, would cut into town activities. However, Caroline's Beauty Salon and the Hoffbrau, both normally quiet on Thursdays, were hubs of activity. Most people, it seemed, were sick of the campaign, but weren't sick of talking about it.

Raymond tried in vain to get Brother Jacob to offer a prayer during the show, but his minister was "extremely busy" with pastoral duties away from town all day. He was finally over his brief stint as celebrity theologian.

Eventually, Cooper turned to his copy of *Book of Famous Prayers*, offering up this petition, yet not revealing the words came from General George Patton:

Graciously hearken to this soldier
who calls upon Thee that, armed with Thy power, I may
advance from victory, and crush the wickedness
of my enemy and establish justice among men.

Though Cooper was not a popular figure among the regulars at Caroline's, most bowed as he prayed.

"He may be a schmuck, but he does have a way with words," Essie Kennemer noted.

Knowing folks on both sides of the political fence would be calling his show that day, Raymond asked Marvin Walsh to man the phones and determine which calls he had "time to take" on the air. Walsh knew to put any Bland supporters "on hold."

At 6:00 p.m., Sarah Hyden-Smith, Iris Long and Juliette Stoughton monitored events from a booth at the 'Brau, where they ordered supper and discussed the events of the day.

It was bound to be a smaller turnout at this week's 7:00 p.m. ballot count, as Thursday night was "Wrestling Night" at the Spring County Fair. This year promised an especially exciting show as stars from the past, including The Sheik, Jerry Lawler, Gorilla

Monsoon, and Dory Funk Jr., highlighted the card.

By 7:00, barely 100 folks gathered in front of the Town Hall for the vote count. Chief Dibble announced, "Due to the smaller turnout this week, we will attempt to allow everyone inside the proceedings." As the crowd filed in, he gruffly added, "There will be no chaos."

Little did he know how prophetic his words would be.

Vera Penrod, election coordinator, addressed the crowd. "Votes cast totaled 764."

An audible mumble rose from the crowd. That was 170 fewer votes than were cast a week earlier. Could most of Juliette's supporters have stayed home, refusing to support either remaining candidate?

"You've got this one in the bag, Raymond!" shouted Elbert Lee Jones from the rear corner of the room.

A quick stare from Chief Dibble stopped Jones in this tracks. He quickly remembered his place.

Silence overtook the room as Vera began her ballot count.

"Cooper!" she roared, looking at the first ballot. "Cooper!" she shouted again.

Pausing as she looked at the next ballot, she lowered her volume. "Cooper," she said. It was starting to look like a landslide for Raymond.

Iris Long shook her head as she tallied the votes on her note pad. She realized this was going to be another long night.

After Raymond received the first seven votes of the ballot count, Iris Long wondered if she was the only voter who cast a ballot for Dick Bland. She knew it was a long shot, but she had hoped some of Juliette's supporters would have heeded her call.

Halfway through the count, Vera Penrod made the decision to call a 10-minute break. After 382 votes had been tallied, Raymond

Cooper led with 205 votes, compared with 177 for "Silver Tongue" Dick Bland. Because it was a run-off election, write-in votes were not allowed.

There was a definite buzz in the VFW section, as Cooper supporters anticipated an overwhelming win. Word also spread throughout the crowd that Dory Funk Jr. had defeated The Sheik at the Spring County Fair using his signature move, the "spinning toe hold." It must have been something, seeing The Sheik scream while begging for mercy.

Marvin Walsh, overcome with emotion, shouted, "It looks like true Americans are carrying the night everywhere!"

As the break approached the 15-minute mark, folks took their places as they sensed history taking place before their eyes. After five more minutes, Chief Dibble approached the microphone, wearing a more menacing look than usual.

"Due to a medical issue, Mrs. Penrod will not be able to continue," Dibble announced. "Diane Curtis is driving her to Spring County Hospital."

A murmur grew throughout the crowd. Suddenly, the election count was a bit less important. Vera was like family to everyone in The Valley.

Dibble went on, "Mrs. Penrod said to tell everyone she would be fine, and she requested that Iris Long take her place counting the ballots."

"What?" exclaimed Elbert Lee Jones.

Earl Goodman had thoughts of his own. "No way!" he shouted.

A sharp glance from Chief Dibble in their direction quickly calmed things down. Goodman was already on thin ice after his remarks on Raymond's show concerning the chief.

Dibble then looked in the direction of Iris, who had been tallying the vote on her own reporter's pad. "Mrs. Long, would you continue the vote count?"

You wouldn't think a hardened news reporter would get nervous, but Iris stammered, shocked by the turn of events. "I don't know. I guess so."

Long took Vera's seat in front of the crowd. Chief Dibble placed the ballot box in front of her, and she nervously withdrew a slip of paper.

"Bland!" she shouted with as much energy as she could muster.

"No way!" shouted Walsh. "It's a fix!"

Dibble had about as much as he could stand. He quickly made his way to Marvin, said a few words only Walsh could hear, then made his way back to the stage. Marvin quickly became unusually subdued.

"Bland," continued Iris. Then, "Bland," again.

You could feel the heat rising from the Cooper section, but no one dared say a word with Dibble at full attention.

As the count continued, the tallies on each side of the board became closer. At one point, Iris stopped to catch her breath.

That's when Beatrice Justice spoke just loud enough for most in the crowd to hear her. "Romans 2, verse 11," was all she said, as if she, too, was out of breath.

Perry Prince, almost to himself, but again loud enough for most to hear, uttered, "Bless her heart," referring to the toll the election was taking on everyone, especially Iris.

With 742 votes tallied, Bland had caught Cooper with 22 ballots left. The room became silent, waiting for Long to continue the count. She wasn't a young woman anymore, and she continued more deliberately.

As those final 22 votes were tallied, Chief Dibble no longer sought to quiet the crowd. With every ballot, there was a roar which grew louder with each slip Iris pulled from the box.

"Cooper!" Iris yelled. Then, "Bland!"

The count went back and forth, much like the match between Gorilla Monsoon and Jerry Lawler taking place at the fairgrounds. Just when Lawler had Monsoon down for the count, a sneaky manager drew the attention of the referee, allowing Gorilla to bite his opponent on the upper arm, instantly freeing himself from the submission hold.

With one ballot remaining, Cooper had 381 votes. Bland had 382.

Would there be a second run-off? Could there really be a tie?

As Dibble again attempted to quiet the crowd, word spread that Lawler and Monsoon fought to a draw in their match. Could the drama in Springfield be foreshadowing the events in Lennox Valley?

Iris pulled the final ballot from the box. Dibble needed try no longer to subdue the crowd. You could have heard a pin drop in the room.

Iris looked at the ballot for what seemed like minutes, but was only a few seconds. Putting her hand to her chest, she read the name on the paper, "Bland."

It took a moment to sink in. Raymond Cooper had been defeated by two votes.

"It's a fix!" screamed Walsh. "Iris Long has fixed this election!"

He couldn't control himself. Marvin would have to deal with Chief Dibble at another time, but he could not hide his emotions.

Like most others, I stayed in the Town Hall for several minutes, realizing I had just witnessed history in the making. This was quite possibly the most exciting night in the history of The Valley . . . so far, and the wrestling in Springfield was almost as exciting.

Chapter Thirty-nine

After Effects

Heaven's Just a Sin Away

The morning following "The Great Valley Run-off" was perhaps the oddest moment of my growing-up years. It was as if we were surrounded by a heavy fog as we began that late August Friday.

The Hoffbrau was filled to capacity, with folks lined up at the door waiting to snag one of the coveted tables. The smell of bacon, eggs and coffee filled the air as voices reached almost deafening proportions.

You could tell who was seated at each table by the conversation. Cooper supporters seemed stunned. Several of them held their heads in their hands. Many wondered if the previous evening had been a bad dream.

Bland supporters were boisterous, laughing and acting as if their mayor had the election "in the bag" all along. At 7:34 a.m., "Silver Tongue" Dick Bland entered the 'Brau, shaking hands with well-wishers and beaming from ear to ear.

It was obvious many, myself included, felt relief the election was behind us. Even though I wasn't old enough to vote, I had been pulled into the drama of the election just like everyone else in The

Valley. It was as if a heavy weight had been lifted, and our town could return to normal, as if things would ever be normal again.

As the morning passed, the conversation shifted from the election results to other matters.

Those at the Town Hall had missed the previous night's wrestling. Tales of heroes and villains filled the air.

Word was beginning to spread that Vera Penrod's quick exit from the ballot count was a result of pneumonia. There was much concern when Mrs. Penrod left her left her election coordinator's post on Thursday night. The good folks of The Valley were thankful she hadn't suffered a heart attack or stroke, but they all knew pneumonia was dangerous, especially for someone of advancing years.

Farmers seemed to be taking a rare morning off to enjoy a late breakfast and a break from the stress of the previous months. I overheard Boyd Sanders telling his companions he was certain he had heard a snap as Dory Funk Jr. tightened his "spinning toe hold" on the Sheik.

It was good to see my community excited about something besides the election. I took a breath and thought about Mary Ann. She was so happy when she received the blue ribbon just two days earlier at the Spring County Fair FFA competition. She and I had exercised our lambs together for months as we prepared for the annual event, and we developed something of a budding romance along the way.

My entry, Archibald, didn't place, but it was just as well. My reward was seeing Mary Ann elated as she hugged Snowflake and then rushed over to hug me.

By lunch, the town was buzzing about other matters. Undoubtedly, the most important was an appearance by Tangi Blevins & the Heavenly Hosts later that evening at the fair. Throughout the day, cassette and CD players were humming the tune "Turn Your Radio On."

Back at the radio station, things weren't quite as lively.

Raymond had canceled his Friday afternoon show, instead airing syndicated network programming. There were stories of UFOs, preachers shouting about sin, and other assorted programming to fill the time.

Elbert Lee Jones, Marvin Walsh, Earl Goodman and Raymond sat around the station conference table in stunned silence for hours, interrupted now and then by an outburst by Marvin or Earl.

"I just don't believe it," Marvin lamented. "I just don't believe it."

Earl chimed in, "It can't be real. It all started when Vera left and that newspaper woman was put in charge."

"You have to demand a recount!" Walsh shouted toward Raymond.

Cooper didn't respond. At 4:30, he stood up and left the building. His followers sat in silence for a few minutes.

At the Hoffbrau, Iris Long sat with Juliette Stoughton.

"What's next for you? You've had quite an experience," Iris said to her new friend.

"You know," Juliette responded, "I think I'll go to the fair. I hear there's a popular singer there tonight. I could use some fun for a change."

The mayoral election seemed a million miles away on Friday night at the Spring County Fair. With "Silver Tongue" firmly entrenched in his role as leader of The Valley for four more years, it was as if the good folks breathed a collective sigh as they caravanned en masse to participate in the most anticipated county fair performance in memory.

I somehow managed to get up the nerve to invite Mary Ann Tinkersley to attend the show with me. I wasn't sure if she was as excited as I was about our first official date. We had been exercising lambs together for the better part of three months, and in my thinking it was just a matter of time before we became "official."

Although Springfield, the county seat, had a much larger population than our town, it seemed as if almost half the crowd was from The Valley. Perhaps the bigger city folks didn't understand the star power of Tangi Blevins, or perhaps they weren't in need of a break as much as we were.

Springfield radio stations had been playing Tangi's biggest hit, "Turn Your Radio On," several times each day during Spring County Fair week. Even Raymond Cooper, firmly entrenched in the battle of his life, had made it a habit to begin each day by playing the song as his station came on the air.

Husbands in their flannel shirts and boots, and wives in their finest jean skirts were dressed for a night on the town. It was probably the biggest date night in years for the folks of my hometown. Even my mom and dad got dressed up for the occasion. I wore my best Levis and a Stetson hat my dad had given me on my previous birthday.

Not everyone had a date. I noticed Juliette Stoughton walking through the fair gate alone as I stood in line to buy a funnel cake for Mary Ann. I figured she was meeting someone, or perhaps she needed a night on her own after the long campaign.

Being new to the area, I guessed Ms. Stoughton probably didn't understand she was participating in one of the biggest nights in Valley history. At the time, I knew nothing about her soulmate and the loneliness she was enduring.

Like every big-time concert, the warm-up act preceded the main event. Little Lori Tolliver wowed the crowd with her banjo playing and pitch-perfect voice. When she belted out "Stand By Your Man," her 12-year-old voice filled the outdoor arena. Her trilogy of sentimental favorites, including "Roses for Mama," "10-4 Teddy Bear," and "Blind Man in the Bleachers," left barely a dry eye among the audience in the folding metal stadium seats.

Being the true showperson she was, she lifted those same spirits with the finest banjo version of "The Devil Went Down to Georgia" heard to this day.

The audience was beside itself as Tangi Blevins & the Heavenly Hosts made their way to the stage. It was years before I realized the irony as she kicked off her performance with a song made famous by father-daughter duo The Kendalls, "Heaven's Just a Sin Away."

In retrospect, it's pretty funny to think about a gospel group, much less a father-daughter duo, singing a song about a sin being so tempting they couldn't help but give in.

In true gospel fashion, the Heavenly Hosts, two 20-something backup singers in mid-length denim skirts with chevron patterns and yellow boots, pointed toward the heavens as they sang, "'cause I belong to Him." Obviously not the "him" the original songwriter had in mind.

Tangi knew how to put on a show, and there was no way she was going to sing her biggest hit until late in her performance, possibly as an encore. She bedazzled the audience. It's no wonder she had such a successful career.

Between songs, she would tell stories about her parents, her children and her beloved husband. She explained how she was "saved" at a revival at the age of 12. There wasn't a dry eye in the audience as she told that story.

Midway through the show, I felt Mary Ann lay her head against my shoulder as Tangi sang the Dolly Parton classic, "I Will Always Love You." That's one song that's guaranteed to bring a couple, young or old, together while it's being sung.

As I looked over toward Mary Ann, I saw Juliette Stoughton from the corner of my eye. It looked like she might be crying. I suppose a love song, sung by a true artist like Tangi Blevins, can do that. I now realize it was probably something else.

A moment later I looked back and she was gone. I figured she'd gone to the concession stand to get a funnel cake. It was several years before I realized how wrong I was about the funnel cake.

Chapter Forty

Soulmates

"Soulmates come and go. Kind of like chameleons."
-Ken Bell

The year 1998 was tough for Juliette Stoughton. Sure, she almost single-handedly ended the political career of would-be mayor Raymond Cooper, was seriously contemplating a protest at the Baptist Church, and made two close friends in Sarah Hyden-Smith and Iris Long. The truth is, however, there were things going on within Juliette her newfound fame couldn't camouflage.

She had nothing against Tangi Blevins, but she just couldn't sit any longer, listening as the pseudo-superstar sang those famous lyrics by Dolly Parton, about bitter-sweet memories. It was like the song was written about Juliette.

Juliette left the fairground stands rapidly, making her way past the ticket booth and vendors selling corn dogs, cotton candy and funnel cakes. She walked quickly, her only thought being how she would soon be anywhere besides there, surrounded by all those happy people.

It's funny how lonely a person can feel, even in a crowd. At that moment, the crowd made Juliette feel even more lonely.

Juliette had always been an avid reader. Ancient history had always been her favorite subject as far back as she could remember. In 1998, she found herself thinking often about something Plato said. "Love is a serious mental disease."

Juliette used to believe Plato was too busy thinking elevated thoughts to understand something as simple as true love. How could anything as wonderful as the love she had with Chris Roadhouse be described as a disease? Finally, she was beginning to understand what he meant.

Finally, nearly out of earshot of the concert, Juliette took a turn in the direction of the fair exit. In just a hundred feet or so, past the Chamber of Commerce display, she would be safe, or so she thought. As she hurried, Juliette kept her eyes on the ground, taking long steps to keep her pace. It was imperative she get to her car and get away from the county fair and all those happy people.

That's when it happened, like a scene from *The Way We Were*, with Robert Redford and Barbra Streisand. The 1970s tale tells the story of two young lovers, torn apart by differences in religion, politics and economic backgrounds.

"Juliette?" the familiar voice said.

At first, Juliette thought she was hearing things. Then, she looked up to see Chris Roadhouse, the man she once considered her soulmate, directly in front of her. He was holding a paper cup and grinning.

"You look great," he said, seemingly as surprised as she was. "I never dreamed I'd run into you here, at a county fair. It doesn't seem like something you'd go for."

"What are you doing here?" Juliette asked. "I mean, I never took you as a 'fair' kind of person, either."

"My company has a booth in the Exhibit Hall," he answered. "You must not have gone in there or you would have noticed. I've been working there quite a bit since the fair began."

He asked how she was.

"I'm fine," she said. The truth was she felt anything but fine at the moment. Over the years, I've learned "fine" is a way people often describe themselves when they are anything but fine.

He told her he saw her name in the newspaper.

"Did you really run for mayor?"

Juliette didn't have much to say. Or perhaps she just couldn't get the words out.

"I was really surprised when I saw that. It didn't seem like something you would do."

He told her he missed her and thought of her a lot. Juliette sensed he might be waiting for her to say the same.

"You know," she answered, "there's probably a lot you don't know about me, Chris. I've changed a lot since you knew me."

Her former soulmate stood in silence for a moment, finally responding, "I guess you're right. I never would have thought you'd come to a fair, much less run for mayor. I guess there's a lot I don't know about you anymore."

After a moment of awkward silence, she spoke. "You know, Chris," she began, "it's been really nice to see you."

"Would you like to get a soda or something?" he asked.

It was one of those defining moments. The kind that comes around rarely in a lifetime.

For a moment, Juliette was tempted to say, "Yes, let's have a soda! Let's get in your car and drive away to anywhere, any place where we can be together."

Juliette had grown a lot in a year, however, and instead answered, "No. Thank you, though. Actually, I was just making my way to the ladies' room so I could get back to the concert."

Chris was surprised by her newfound interest in country gospel music.

"Are you sure?" he asked.

Yes, she was sure. As she stood there, looking at the man she once considered her soulmate, the man she had thought she would spend the rest of her life with, she was sure.

"It was nice seeing you," Juliette said just before turning toward the ladies' room just 20 feet to her right. "I really should get going. It was nice seeing you."

Surprised by her response, Chris wasn't sure what to say. He searched for something, anything profound to say as she began to walk away.

"Call me any time you want to talk," he blurted out. "I mean that. Any time."

Juliette knew she would never call. She suddenly realized she was in the mood to see the rest of the concert. Upon entering the stand area, she noticed Iris Long taking pictures for the newspaper. She slipped in beside her new friend.

"I'm surprised you made it here," Iris noted with a friendly laugh. "I didn't take you for a 'fair' kind of person, or a gospel music fan."

They both laughed.

"Well," Juliette replied with a grin, "I wanted to see what all the excitement was about."

She was just in time, as Tangi reappeared on stage for her final encore. As she listened to Tangi and her backup group sing "Turn Your Radio On," she remembered a quote by her favorite modern author, J.S.B. Morse, who wrote about a broken heart being part of growing. She suddenly appreciated what he was writing about when he said a broken heart was necessary to appreciate real love when it comes along.

"Is it what you thought it would be like?" Iris asked, referring to the county fair and concert.

"Oh, it's better. Much better," Juliette answered with a smile.

Iris thought for a moment, thinking about the past year, before saying, "I'm glad. Maybe things are finally turning around for you."

"I think they already are," Juliette said to her new friend. "I think they already are."

To be continued . . .

Dedication

Dedicated to my friends:

Iris Long, Helen Walker and Jessie Orr Gouge

Helen Walker **Iris Long** **Jessie Orr Gouge**

Watch for the next book in the
Good Folks of Lennox Valley series,
coming Fall 2017

The Good Folks
of Lennox Valley
Fall 1998

by Kevin Slimp

Market
Square
BOOKS

MarketSquareBooks.com